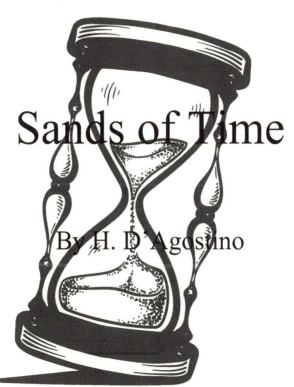

Sands of Time

By H. D'Agostino

Sands of Time
Sands of Time

H. D'Agostino

Copyright © May 2019 by Heather D'Agostino

All Rights Reserved. This book may not be reproduced, scanned, or distributed in any printed or electronic form without permission from the author. Please do not participate in or encourage piracy of copyrighted materials in violation of the author's rights. All characters and storylines are the property of the author and your support and respect is appreciated. The characters and events portrayed in this book are fictitious. Any similarity to real persons, living or dead, is coincidental and not intended by the author. The following story contains mature themes, profanity, and sexual situations. It is intended for adult readers.

Cover Design by Pink Ink Designs

Editing by Kellie Montgomery

Photography by Shauna Kruse @Kruse Images

Cover Model: Ryan Harmon

Table of Contents

Chapter 1…..5

Chapter 2…..12

Chapter 3…..22

Chapter 4…..32

Chapter 5…..43

Chapter 6…..49

Chapter 7…..58

Chapter 8…..68

Chapter 9…..76

Chapter 10…..86

Chapter 11…..96

Chapter12…..105

Chapter 13…..116

Chapter 14…..127

Chapter 15…..137

Chapter 16…..146

Chapter 17…..157

Chapter 18…..167

Sands of Time

Chapter 19…..178

Chapter 20…..186

Chapter 21…..196

Chapter 22…..204

Chapter 23…..214

Epilogue…..218

Sands of Time Playlist…..223

Other Works by H. D'Agostino…..224

Acknowledgements…..227

About the Author…..229

Chapter 1

5 years ago...

Kaitlyn

Timing is everything. It affects every choice we make in our lives. It impacts our relationships, and the future depends on it. We don't realize it when it's happening, but every choice, every moment, every feeling comes back to something we said or did sometimes years before.

Leaving Crescent Moon Beach was one of the hardest things I had ever done, but I think coming back now is even harder. I met Eli Baker in French class. His seat was behind mine, and he used his lack of understanding as a tool to talk to me. We bonded in a way no one really understood at the age of sixteen. It didn't take long before our friendship turned into something else, and I destroyed it.

On graduation day as my classmates and I were putting on our caps and gowns, Eli was busy telling me about how great our summer was going to be before college. What he didn't know was I wasn't spending the summer at home. I'd been given the opportunity of a lifetime, a chance to study culinary arts in Paris, and I was going to take it.

That afternoon as we sat on the beach in our spot, I broke his heart for the first time. I stared straight at the water as I let my confession flow from my lips. I was leaving at the end of the week. I was sorry, and I'd be back in a couple years, but I needed to take this chance because I wasn't sure I'd ever have another one. This was my moment, a moment to shine.

"I don't know why this is so hard," I muttered under my breath. I hated flying. I hated it so much that I usually took a Xanax before I climbed on a plane. Not today though, and I'm cursing myself every time this tin can hits a small pocket of air. I'd been sitting here for almost eleven hours, and I was counting the minutes until we touched down.

"Please fasten your seatbelts," the airline attendant's voice came over the speaker. "We're making our descent now and should be on the ground shortly." I sighed as I leaned back into my seat. My hands were white knuckled on the armrest, and I think the woman beside me was just as ready to get away from me as I was to get off.

When the plane touched down, I released a deep breath. I was home. This was the first time I'd set foot on American soil in five years. My parents had come to Europe several times, I'd never had the time to come visit them until now. Christmas was my favorite time of year. I loved the smells as much as the sights. Part of what got me interested in cooking were the pastries that this little bakery down the road put in their window at Christmas. Eli and I would stop in and pick out one to share every time we walked by.

Eli... I wondered what he was doing. When I left, I had promised to come back, but one thing led to another, and I ended up staying in France. I'd always dreamed of running my own kitchen and learning from some of the best chefs in the industry was a dream come true. We'd kept in touch for the first year, sending letters to each other, but as time passed the letters became fewer and the time between them grew. I'd finally given up when he sent me a 'Dear John' letter. I never thought my heart would break while I was doing what I loved, but I was wrong. Eli had always been a part of me. He was my first real boyfriend, my first kiss, my first everything. Even though we'd been apart for months, it still hurt.

As I stood in line at customs, I wondered what he was doing now. Did he open his own place like we'd always talked about? Was he married yet? Was he even still in Crescent Moon Beach? "Miss?" The man behind the counter jostled me out of my memory. I handed over my passport as I rambled off my reason for visiting and waited for the stamp of approval. I'd planned to visit for a week, and then I had to go back. My boss had been generous with the week off. It was very busy this time of year with the holiday and working as his sous chef had been no easy feat.

"Enjoy your stay." He handed me back my passport, and I grabbed my carry on as I made my way to baggage claim. After picking up my luggage, and checking in to get my rental, I began the drive to my parents' house. It was evening and as the highway turned into the narrow beach road that led to my childhood home, I began to feel those comforting feelings wrap me in their familiarity. It didn't matter how far you went or how long you were gone, home would always be home and I was finally back.

ooooooooo

"Katie Girl!" my dad called as I stepped out of my car and took a big whiff of sea air.

"Hey Dad." I smiled. I popped the trunk to get my bags and was rounding the car when Mom appeared.

"Kait," she sighed as if it were a relief that I was home.

"Hey Mom." I grinned as I heaved the suitcase onto the ground. Dad rushed over to grab it, but I swung my arms around his neck before he could. "I missed you guys. Phone calls just aren't enough." I buried my nose in the crook of my dad's neck and sniffed. His aftershave was the same as I remembered. It was familiar, and that small piece of the past made everything better. Don't get me wrong, I love my life, but I miss my past too.

"Let's get you inside," Mom chided from a few steps away. "I have the kettle on. We can have some tea."

"Sounds good." I smiled as I followed them up the stairs of my childhood home.

When I stepped through the door, I couldn't help but grin. In the corner, was the biggest tree I'd ever seen. It was covered in lights from top to bottom, but no ornaments adorned it.

"We were waiting for you." My dad leaned in. "We haven't been able to do this with you in so long."

I pressed my lips together to keep from tearing up. I missed these traditions too. I missed so much, but you don't realize it when you're away. "Thanks." I sniffed as I turned to take in the rest of the room. My nutcracker collection was still lining the mantel, and the nativity that Mom and I painted when I was little was set up on a small table in the corner. "I can't believe you still put all this out." I turned to look at where Mom was pouring tea into three Santa mugs.

"Why? Just because you left, we didn't change." She offered a small smile.

"I know, but don't you want something more... I don't know, grown up?" I tipped my head to the side.

"I like things just like they are," Dad echoed Mom's sentiment. "Not much has changed around here." He lifted a shoulder as he lowered himself into the same brown chair he's had for as long as I can remember.

"What do you mean?" I took the Santa mug from my mom when she offered it and blew gently on the steam.

"We're still hosting our Christmas party." She grinned at me.

"Really?" I was a little too excited for being twenty-three. You would have thought that I was still twelve.

"Yep. We put it off to a later date this year because we knew you were coming. Your mom was hoping that you'd do the cooking." Dad winked.

"Is that why you wanted me to come? So you could get free catering?" I laughed as I sipped my tea.

"You figured us out." Mom laughed as she moved over beside the tree and pulled a box from behind it. "Now come help me." She nudged the box to the side as she moved over to the stereo and flicked it on. Christmas music filled the air, and my heart swelled. This was what I'd been missing for the last five years. I'd had a tree. I'd had the music, and the food, and the parties, but I hadn't had them. Henri had done his best to give me a Crescent Moon Christmas each year, but nothing compared to having my mom and dad with me to celebrate and I had no idea how I was going to go back home in a week.

We spent the rest of the night decorating the tree and reminiscing about Christmases past. I told them about Paris during the holidays, and they filled me in on how nothing's really changed. Their big news was the Walmart that went in a few months ago, and the restoration of the wooden coaster down at the amusement park. I heard about who had a baby, and who got married. They told me about anything and everything except Eli. I didn't ask because it didn't really matter. I had Henri, and nothing going on with Eli was going to change that.

When we finally went to sleep, the sun was starting to rise. I'd assured them I'd be ok, but I knew the jetlag was going to get to me too soon. I crashed with the promise that I'd cook them a real French meal as soon as I woke up and went to the store. I didn't know it then, but the consequences of this trip had already been set in motion, and it was just a matter of time before everything came crashing together… literally.

Chapter 2

Kaitlyn

When I finally dragged myself out of bed the next morning, it wasn't really morning. The sun was on it's way down, and I realized I'd slept most of the day away. I felt terrible that I'd wasted one of my days sleeping, but my body didn't care. It was tired. I rubbed the sleep from my eyes as I made my way from my room out to the kitchen.

"Afternoon sunshine." Mom smiled as she busied herself in the kitchen. There was flour everywhere and the smell of cinnamon, lemon, and cherries filled the air. "I didn't want to wake you. Did you sleep ok?"

"Yeah." I glanced around at the kitchen. "What are you making?"

"My famous tarts." She leaned down and pulled a pan from the oven. "A few different cookies, and then a pie."

"I could have helped, you know." I reached for the coffee pot.

"I know, but I wanted to let you sleep. You cook for work every day. This is your vacation." She swatted my hand as I tried to reach for a scrap of dough that was near the edge of the counter.

"That's different. I like helping you." I poured my coffee and moved to the side opposite her. As I pulled out a chair, my phone chimed with a message.

Henri: Glad you got in ok. Have a great time. Sorry I couldn't join you.

Me: Thanks. I understand.

"If you really want to help, you could make a run to the store." Mom smiled sheepishly.

"I can do that." I nodded as sipped my coffee. "Just make me a list. I'll go throw some clothes on real quick." I hopped down and headed back to my room with my coffee in hand. The least I could do is run a few errands. This would also give me a chance to grab what I needed to cook for them. I wanted to cook something nice for dinner. I needed to show them what I'd been perfecting all these years away.

I quickly changed into some jeans and a sweater before pulling my hair up into a messy bun and slipping on a pair of boots. After swiping on a little gloss and some mascara, I grabbed my purse, and made my way back out to where my mom was pulling another tray of tarts from the oven.

"Here ya go." She handed the list over. "Take your time. I don't need that stuff until tomorrow's baking adventure."

"Be back in a little bit." I waved before slipping into my coat and heading outside. The breeze blowing off the ocean was crisp, but it was great to be back.

oooooooo

Eli

"Why am I always the one to buy the food?" I glared over at my best friend, Jackson. I'd invited him over to my place again for dinner. It had become a regular thing over the last year. When he'd lost his wife and daughter, I'd tried to help out as much as I could. He threw himself into the restaurant we co-owned though and pretty much ignored the pain. The last couple of months seem to be getting better though. He's started to smile again, and we've been having guys' night after we close at least once a week.

"Because you're the one who cooks," he called out somewhere in the back. I was getting out early tonight. It was slow, and the chef I'd hired was working out great. I was finally able to cut my hours back. Jackson never cut back. He had a cot in his office where he slept on more than one occasion. Sometimes I wondered if he even left to shower.

"Just because I cook doesn't mean I have to buy," I grumbled.

"I'll bring the beer." He leaned his head out from where he was hiding.

"Fine." I rolled my eyes. "Steaks will be ready about six, I think."

"See you then." He waved before ducking back to what he was doing.

I grumbled some more as I made my way out to my car. The sun was setting just over the water, and the winter breeze whipped my hair around as I pulled my coat tighter. The drive to the store was quick, and when I pulled in, the lot was almost full. It figured that it would be busy. Christmas was just a week away, and everyone had waited until the last minute to get what they needed for their parties and dinners.

I shook my head in annoyance as I climbed from my car and made my way inside. The store was bustling with patrons grabbing baskets and pushing half-filled carts down the near bare aisles. I ducked around a family arguing over turkeys, a few kids begging for candy, and made my way to the meat counter. I had planned to grill steaks. It was kinda our thing, mine and Jackson's. We'd sit on my deck and drink beer while we talked about our nonexistent dating life. Don't get me wrong, there have been women, just no one to write home about.

I stopped by the strip steaks and began my search just as I was jostled by the person next to me.

"Oh, excuse me!" came a startled voice. I jerked my gaze to where the offender had bumped into me only to see a set of wide startled eyes blinking up. I'm sure I mirrored her expression as the last person I ever expected to see stared back at me.

"Kait?" I blinked a few times just to make sure I wasn't seeing things.

"Eli." It came out as a whisper as the basket she had on her arm fell to the ground. "Oh no!" she yelped.

I leaned down and grabbed it, handing it back to her. "What are you doing here?" I had so many questions, and of course the stupidest one was what came out.

She smiled that wicked smile that had tempted me to do so much in the past before laughing and dipping her chin toward her basket. "Shopping."

"That was dumb." I shook my head. "I mean, what are you doing here, in Crescent Moon again?" I began searching the area with my eyes. I had to be getting 'punked'. I hadn't seen this woman in five years. The last time we were in the same room, she was telling me she was leaving for culinary school. The last communication I'd gotten was her boasting about studying under a French chef.

"I'm visiting my parents," her voice dipped. It wavered a little before she bit down on her lip and blinked up at me. A myriad of emotions played over her face.

"Wow!" I breathed out. "This is just…wow."

"How have you been?" She shifted the weight of the basket.

"Good. I've been good." I felt my phone vibrate in my pocket at that moment, and it made me remember what I'd come here to do. "One sec." I held up my finger as I pulled my cell from my pocket and typed out a quick text to Jackson cancelling our plans. "Sorry." I grimaced as I slipped it back into place. "You wanna get a drink somewhere, and talk?" I glanced around. I did not want to let this woman out of my sight. The years seem to stretch the more I thought about them, and I didn't know how much time I had before she slipped away again.

"Sure." She shrugged. "I have a few more things to grab, and then I'll meet you in the parking lot?" She tipped her head to the side.

"Sounds good." I smiled as I grabbed a pack of steaks, not even caring if they were good ones or not.

After paying for my groceries, I made my way outside. I tossed my bags into the trunk of my car just as Kaitlyn was coming out the door. "I'll follow you," she called out as she clicked a key fob that caused a set of taillights a few spaces down from me to flash. I waved in acknowledgment as I climbed in and cranked the engine.

The logical thing would be to take her to Anchor Bay. I mean, I own it but I wasn't ready to share her yet. Instead, I began to drive to this little dive bar a few blocks from my house. The Silver Crane was tucked away and only a few locals frequented it.

"This looks interesting." Kaitlyn laughed as she climbed from her car. I missed that laugh. It shot right to my heart.

"It's better on the inside." I chuckled as I made my way to the door. The old wood creaked as I pulled it open and stepped aside. There was a long bar that ran along one side. Small tables filled one end, and a pool table and dart board were at the other. It was dark inside with neon beer signs providing the light. Kaitlyn smiled back at me as she meandered between the tables, stopping at one in the far corner.

"This ok?" She glanced back as she started to take off her coat. I nodded in acceptance as I attempted not to stare. She looked just as beautiful as I remembered. Tall, lean, with big, brown doe eyes. Her mouth turned up slightly on one side as she caught me staring. "I can turn if you like," she teased.

"Sorry." I muttered an apology. "I just... I can't believe you're here."

"Me either." It was an almost embarrassed laugh.

"So why now? Why come back?" I tried to not sound bitter, but I couldn't help it. I'd loved her, and she left me.

She'd broken my heart, and I didn't even get a phone call.

"My parents asked me to, and I was able to get some time off." She shrugged as if it was no big deal. "How have you been?"

"Same." I lifted a shoulder just as the bartender stopped by our table and placed two beers in front of us. I came here enough that I didn't really need to order.

"Are you cooking?" She reached out and touched my arm. Small shockwaves zinged from where she touched me, and I almost recoiled. I forced myself not to though because I yearned to feel that again. When Kaitlyn left the last time, she took my heart with her. I hadn't had a reaction from a woman since.

"Yep." I jerked my head as I took a gulp of beer. I needed to keep my mouth busy so I didn't try to kiss her. "You?"

"I thought you knew." A confused look washed over her. "I work as the sous chef at Chez Mari. When I finished studying with Henri, he took me on as his sous chef. I've been there since I left." She pressed her lips together.

"You're happy then." It came out as more of a statement than a question.

She smiled. "Most of the time, yes. What about you?"

"Am I happy?" I paused to think about it. It really depended on when you asked. Most days I was as happy as I could be, working crazy hours with no woman in my life. "Sure. I've accomplished most of what I wanted in life. There are a few things I'd change, but hell, we can't have it all. Can we?" I picked up the beer and let it run down my throat. My hands were itching to touch her. She had matured over the years. The thin frame that once looked so fragile was now curvy and more supple. "How long are you staying?"

"I go home on New Year's Eve." She sipped her beer as her eyes danced around the room. She glanced at her watch. "I'd love to catch up more, but I need to get back. I promised my parents I'd cook dinner for them tonight."

I curled my fingers where they rested on my thighs. Every instinct was telling me to stop her. I needed more time. She was the one who got away, and I was getting another chance. "What are you doing tomorrow night?" I was grasping at straws here.

"Nothing." She smiled sweetly.

"How about you come by the old Anchor Bay Bar and I'll show you what I do?" I reached for my wallet and tossed a few bills on the bar to cover our tab.

"Is that where you work?" Her smile grew bigger.

"Something like that." I chuckled. She didn't need to know that I co-owned the place yet. I wanted to show her that I'd done well for myself too. I wasn't some line cook in a chain somewhere. I'd designed and implemented a menu that I carried out daily. Choosing specials and pairing wines was something I did too.

"Ok." She stood and began slipping her coat on. "I have to help my mom tomorrow, but I could come by around eight. Would that work?"

"Sounds like a plan." I too stood and slipped my coat on before leading the way outside. The wind was blowing harder at this point, signaling a storm coming in. We both pulled our coats tighter around us as we headed to our respective cars. "I'll see you tomorrow." I waved as I climbed in. I needed to get home and analyze this. Kaitlyn coming back even if only for a visit was not something that I'd planned for. What if she felt the same way I did? What if this was a second chance? What if I could convince her to stay? I needed her to stay and figuring out how to make that happen was going to be my mission this week. I couldn't let her slip through my fingers again.

Chapter 3

Eli

"I'll close tonight, ok?" I stuck my head in Jackson's office where he was entering payroll into the computer.

"You close next week. Why do you want to take on one of my nights? Do you want something from me?" He closed the laptop and leaned back in his chair.

"No. I just thought I'd be nice. You seem tired." I lifted a shoulder as I stepped through the door.

"You're up to something." He pointed at me before his face split into a grin. "Who's the girl?"

"There is no girl." I rolled my eyes at him. He knew me so well. I did not want to explain Kaitlyn to him. We talked about everything, but her.

"Right. The last time you wanted me out of here was because you were bringing a girl here to impress."

I took a deep breath and shook my head. "Fine. I met someone the other night. I wanted to cook for her."

"I knew it." He stood up and laughed.

"Shut up," I grumbled. "You're such a girl. Can I close for you or not?"

"Fine. A night out early? I'm game, just don't fuck her in the kitchen or on my desk." He narrowed his eyes at me.

"Don't be an asshole." I huffed as I turned to head back to the kitchen. I was almost finished prepping for dinner and I wanted to take stock of what I could fix for Kaitlyn. She was coming late, so I was thinking dessert.

As the day wore on, business picked up. With the holidays coming we were getting more and more business. It seemed that after baking all day, people wanted someone else to cook their meals for them. Jackson had left me alone as he ran the front of the house, and I stayed in the back. When it finally started to slow down, he left as promised. I've never gotten him out of the place as fast as I did tonight and I'm wondering if he has a lady he's hoping to meet up with too.

By the time Kaitlyn arrived, we were slowing down for the night. My kitchen had been running flawlessly, and our assistant manager was floating from table to table. I rounded the corner to head to the front door just as she was coming through it. The sight of her took my breath away. She looked both beautiful, and dangerous at the same time.

"Hey." She waved as she came to a stop by the hostess stand.

"You made it." I waved in return. "I got this, Jen." I stopped the hostess as she started to pull a menu out.

"Sure thing, Boss." She smiled at me. Jen had made it no secret that she wanted me. I'm sure I could get whatever my dick desired from her if I asked. She'd probably follow me out to my car right now.

"Boss?" Kaitlyn's eyes widened as she moved closer. I could smell her perfume. It was a mix of cinnamon and vanilla and completely Kaitlyn. "Do you manage this place?"

"I co-own this place." I puffed out my chest with pride as I reached for her. "Come with me." I stepped up beside her and gently began to lead her to the bar by placing my palm on her lower back. She didn't even flinch which was a good sign. If she wasn't pulling away from me yet, then I still had a chance. "I'm glad you came out tonight."

"Me too." She slipped into the booth that I stopped beside. "I can't believe you own this place. It's amazing, Eli!" Her voice was filled with awe and pride, and I knew she was being honest. We'd talked about opening a restaurant together when we were in high school. It was a dream we shared. I always thought we'd go to culinary school together, and then we'd get some dive and turn it around. I'd kept that dream alive, but Kaitlyn hadn't.

"Thanks. Guess one of us followed our dreams." I didn't mean for them to, but the words came out with a little edge. I was angry, and as much as I didn't want to waste time being mad at her, I couldn't help it.

"That's not fair." She leaned back in the booth as she crossed her arms. "Just because I don't own a restaurant doesn't mean that I'm not happy. I've been featured in Good Bites Magazine, Eli. I've seen success too. Don't judge my life when you haven't been a part of it in a long time."

Rage. Rage was what I felt. "I haven't been a part of it because of you! You chose to cut me out, not the other way around." I gritted my teeth as I glared at her. This wasn't how I saw this night going, but nothing about her coming back was normal. I reined in my temper as I shook my head and stood. "I'm sorry. I didn't mean for that to come out like that. I'm just... never mind."

"Maybe I should go." She started to put her coat back on, but I reached out to stop her.

"Please don't. You haven't seen my kitchen." I flashed a grin at her, the grin that I'd used on more than one occasion to get what I wanted from her.

"Fine." She sighed. "I'll stay, but just because I want to see what you're cooking with." She tried to keep from laughing, but she couldn't, and as the giggle escaped her lips, her eyes scanned down my front.

"I'm cooking with some state of the art equipment, equipment that you've probably only dreamed about."

"I doubt that. I've seen a lot of equipment in my day." She laughed again before slipping from the booth. "Lead the way." Her hand swept out and all I could think about was the other equipment I had that I'd like to show her.

ooooooooo

Kaitlyn

I don't know why I thought meeting him here was a good idea. I guess I was more curious than anything. Leaving him behind was one of the hardest things I've ever done, until this. When I came here, I thought maybe it was close to where he lived, or maybe he was the chef here. Him owning this place was the last thing I expected. When I came through the door and saw him standing there, I almost tripped over my own feet. He looked so different than he did the night before. His hair was styled neatly, and he was dressed in a black button down and black slacks. The collar was open, and the cuffs were rolled up his forearms. His lip curved up as he smiled at me, and I was done for. The argument though was not expected. I knew he'd been mad when we first broke up, but that was five years ago. We were kids then, and I figured he would have moved on.

"So how long have you owned this place?" I looked around as I followed Eli down a narrow hallway.

"Almost three years." He opened a door and motioned inside. "You can put your things in the office. They'll be safe in there."

I tossed my purse and coat onto a chair near the door before stepping out of the way and letting him close the door. "Kitchen's this way." He motioned behind me, and I stepped back to let him pass. When we rounded the corner, my mouth dropped open in awe. The kitchen was beautiful. Much more than I expected for a place like this. I figured he would have used the old equipment, but no. There was a huge stove, a flat top, and a prep area big enough for three people to work at together. Several ovens lined the back, and a large butcher block was stocked with knives of every size.

"How many cooks do you have?" I figured he didn't cook often since he was the boss.

"I have one head chef, and three prep cooks. Depending on business, I prep at times. When we first started out, I had a five-man team. It was a lot of work." He sighed as the two cooks he had working tonight began the nightly cleaning. "You can leave that area." He pointed to a spot behind us. "The top oven too." The man he was pointing to nodded and then grinned.

"Have a good night, Boss." He tossed a towel on the counter before untying his apron and stuffing it in a laundry basket.

"Same to you, Sam." Eli waved before turning to me. "Still like your sweets?"

"Of course." I tipped my head to one side. "I live in France. I'm a trained pastry chef."

"Have a seat." He pointed to the counter.

"On the counter? That's not sanitary." I scoffed.

"It's my restaurant, and I said to sit. I'll clean it when I'm finished." He shrugged before walking toward the huge refrigerator. When he emerged, he had an arm full of eggs, milk, and butter. He set them on the counter before grabbing sugar, cinnamon, and a few other ingredients.

"Are you making what I think you're making?" I licked my lips as I stared at the spot on the counter where he was cracking the eggs. He expertly placed each egg in the bowl, one handed I might add, and began to whisk them together.

"What do you think I'm making?" he teased as his face remained stoic.

"Nothing." I feigned indifference.

I began to swing my feet back and forth as I watched Eli in fascination. We played around when we were younger. We never cooked at the level we do now and watching him move with ease around his kitchen like he was born in it was awe inspiring. His face held deep concentration while his hand effortlessly mixed until he began to pour his concoction into two ramekins. He set them in a roasting pan and pushed it into the oven before coming to stand in front of me.

"I gotta go get the torch. Think you can keep an eye on that for me?" He winked.

"Uh... sure," I stammered. Why did being here like this affect me so. Awareness zinged through me, and my heart thudded in my chest. I swallowed as I watched him turn and waltz away like he was completely unaffected by me.

When he returned, he glanced in the oven before coming to stand in front of me. "I haven't had anything this pretty in my kitchen since," he tapped his chin, "well, ever."

"You haven't had a girlfriend?" I was shocked. "In five years?"

"I didn't say that." He glanced at me and then back at the stove. "I haven't brought one in here, ever. You're the first person that doesn't work here to come in here."

"I'm impressed." I pressed my lips together and nodded before my mouth curved into a smile. I lifted my chin toward the oven. "It should be ready."

"You think so?" He turned toward the oven but didn't move.

"Crème Brulee takes forty-five minutes to bake give or take a minute or two." I shrugged and smiled impishly.

Eli threw his head back and laughed before striding to the oven. The next thing I knew, he was carrying the pan towards me. He used a mitt and grabbed each ramekin and slipped them into the blast chiller before turning back to me. "Guess you were right." He chuckled.

"It happens on occasion." I shrugged before looking away. Every time I looked at him I felt what I'd suppressed years ago stir, and the more it stirred the more it wanted to come to surface, only I couldn't let it. I was going back to Paris in a week. Back to my life, one that I didn't share with Eli.

After torching the sugar, Eli brought the ramekins over to where I was sitting. "Dig in." He motioned to the spoon he'd set on the counter beside me. I dipped it in and brought the custard to my lips. The moment it hit my tongue, I groaned. It tasted so good, as good as if I made it myself.

"Mmm." I sighed and closed my eyes.

"I miss hearing that." Eli muttered, causing my eyes to fly open. When they did, he was staring at my mouth. His hands were gripping the countertop so tightly that his knuckles were white. His tongue slipped out to wet his lips before he leaned closer. I couldn't do this. I needed to stop it now.

"I gotta go." I pushed my dessert to the side before scrambling off the countertop. "This was great, but I have somewhere I have to be." I refused to look at him. I knew by the silence in the room that I'd confused him. I'd come here and let him cook for me. I willingly flirted with him, and now I was bolting. I rushed out of the kitchen to get my coat and purse.

When I came back down the hallway, I could see him still in the kitchen. His back was to the door, his hands splayed out on the counter with his head dropped between his shoulders. I tightened my arms around my middle as I rushed silently out to my car. Coming here was a bad idea, and I needed to go home and remind myself why. I couldn't go through this again. We weren't even together, but as I drove away from The Anchor Bar every part of me began to break. My heart was being torn in two and Eli didn't even know why.

Chapter 4

Eli

"How was your date last night?" Jackson stood smirking at me while I chopped vegetables for the Manhattan Chowder today.

"I don't want to talk about that, and it wasn't a date," I grumbled as the knife came down harder.

"That good, huh?" Jackson chuckled.

My head lifted in his direction as my eyes shot daggers. "If I wanted feedback from you, I would have asked. Now go bother someone else." I growled.

"Sorry I asked." He held his hands up in surrender.

He stood there just watching as I took my aggression out on the cutting board in front of me. I knew I had no right to be upset. Kaitlyn and I weren't a couple. We weren't even friends. We weren't anything. I was stupid to think that inviting her here would change that. "She ran out of here so fast last night that she created a breeze," I muttered as I continued to dice the vegetables and place them in the huge pot behind me.

"Why?" Jackson moved closer and propped himself against the wall.

"Don't you think I would do something about that if I knew why?" I shook my head as my mouth twisted in aggravation.

"Have you talked to her today?" he prodded.

"No. I've called her a few times. It went to voicemail." I sighed. Jackson didn't know that she hadn't given her number to me. I snagged her phone last night and called myself. I don't even know if she knows it's my number.

"Do you know where she's staying? Maybe you should try to woo her. Bring her flowers and shit. Women love that kinda thing." He wagged his brows like he was an expert or something. Asshole hasn't had a relationship since he lost his wife. I haven't pushed him, but she was the only one he dated that I knew of, and now he wanted to act like he was the expert on women.

"Yes, I know where she's staying, and this woman doesn't like that sort of thing…or surprises for that matter," I mumbled as I tossed the last little bit of carrots I was chopping into the pot.

"So, what's the plan?" He chuckled.

"What makes you think I have a plan?" I shook my head as I pushed by him and headed toward the office. I didn't want to talk about this with my subordinates within earshot.

"One: You always have a plan, and two: I've never seen you so twisted up over a woman before." He laughed harder as he followed me into the office.

"She's not just some woman." I sighed as I dropped dramatically into the chair in the corner. It was the one where Kaitlyn left her coat last night, and it still smelled slightly of her perfume. "She's the one." I placed my arm over my eyes and groaned. I was tired. I'd spent most of last night analyzing what had happened. I'd thought things were going well until she bolted. Maybe I was reading her signals wrong. Maybe I'd been reading her wrong all along and that's why it was such a shock when she left the first time.

"Oooh." Jackson's eyes widened. "Listen man," he paused as he scratched his chin, "I don't know her, but I know you, and I know you need to talk to her. How long is she staying in town?"

"Til New Year's," I muttered.

"Then you need to make time to talk to her. I can handle tonight. We're closing early anyway. It's Christmas Eve. Go talk to her. Tell her how you feel. Put it all out there, man." He moved closer and clapped me on the shoulder. "I'm here if she shoots you down."

"Thanks for the vote of confidence." I rolled my eyes as I watched him walk out of the office. He was right. I needed to talk to her, but I didn't want to barge in on Christmas Eve. I knew she'd be with her family, and they deserved time with her too. Maybe I could wait until after Christmas. I still had a few days, but who was I kidding. I needed to see her. I needed to know what I did wrong, and if I even had a chance. It was Christmas, and if I was going to get a miracle, then it would be tonight.

oooooooooo

Kaitlyn

When I woke up I almost forgot that it was Christmas Eve. I'd spent the night before tossing and turning and stressing over the fact that I'd almost let Eli kiss me. I could tell by the way he looked at me that he was confused and hurt. What surprised me the most was the fact that he hadn't run after me. Five years ago, he wouldn't have let me leave like that. He would have run out into the parking lot and forced me to tell him what was wrong. I guess that's what happens when you walk away from someone… they stop trying.

I climbed out of bed and padded down the hall toward the kitchen, letting my nose lead me. The smell of fresh baked cinnamon rolls was wafting down the hall, and the sound of softly playing Christmas music accompanied it.

"Morning Katie girl." My dad smiled as he sat in his favorite chair drinking his morning coffee. The tree was lit up behind him, and a fire crackled in the fireplace. It was unseasonably cold this year, and I was thankful I'd packed my flannel pajamas.

"Morning, Daddy." I smiled as I rubbed my tired eyes.

"Looks like Santa needs to bring you some sleep. Is the time difference still messing you up?" He rocked forward as if he was going to get up and I brushed him off.

"No. Just a lot on my mind." I sighed as I made my way into the kitchen. I opened the oven and sniffed the cinnamon rolls before pouring myself a cup of coffee.

"Almost ready." Mom smiled as she came over to hug me. "You look exhausted. Maybe a party isn't such a good idea."

"But it's tradition." I frowned. "You just said yesterday that everyone was excited to come because I was here this year."

"They are, but it's Christmas and I'm thinking I don't want to share you." She smiled as she cupped my cheek.

"Oh, Momma." I set my coffee cup down and wrapped my arms around her. "I promise I'll come back sooner next time."

"So if you're really up for a party, then what's causing these dark circles? Is it Henri? Is he making you worry about work while you're on vacation?" She stepped back and crossed her arms over her chest.

"No, Momma." I blew out a breath as I sat down at the table. "It's Eli Baker."

Silence filled the room, and then her footsteps stopped behind me. "I haven't heard that name in a long time. Why is he twisting you up like this?"

"I ran into him the other night at the store. That friend I was meeting last night was him. He invited me to his restaurant. Did you know he owned The Anchor Bay bar?" I glanced up at her face before going back to my coffee.

"I did." She nodded. "He's done really well for himself, him and his friend, Jackson."

"Well, I think he thinks that I still have feelings for him." I chewed my lip and refused to look up at her. I couldn't stomach the judgement that I thought would be coming next.

"Do you?" Her voice was soft, and she squeezed my shoulder.

"It doesn't matter if I do. You know I can't be with him. I live in Paris. My entire life is there. I'm going back to it in a few days." My head dropped as I raked my hands through my hair. "This sucks," I muttered. Why did things have to be like this? If I'd come home a few years ago, my life could be different, but it's not.

"I know baby. You can't change the past. All you can do is learn from it." She moved in front of me. "Are you happy?"

"Yes. I mean, I think I am." I glanced out the window at the blue sky. It was a crisp winter day. "Why wouldn't I be?"

"I don't know." She moved back to the stove to pull the cinnamon buns out. "For someone that's happy, you sure seem sad."

"I'm happy, Momma." I turned to where she was plating a bun. "It's Christmas Eve and we're having a party."

oooooooo

Eli

I don't know what I was thinking when I agreed to come here. When Jackson told me that Kaitlyn's dad had called the bar looking for me, I was curious. When he called back and invited me to their annual party, I almost choked on the water I was sipping. Now I'm sitting in their driveway, staring at a house covered in Christmas lights and full of people. I hadn't been to one of their parties since Kait and I were in high school. We used to sneak alcohol from her dad's liquor cabinet out onto their deck and get drunk while we fooled around. The last time I was here was the day she told me she was leaving. I'd come to a graduation party that ended up being a breakup for us.

"You can do this," I whispered under my breath before shoving open the door and climbing out. With a bottle of wine tucked against my side, I took the front steps two at a time. I rang the doorbell and stepped back, waiting for what seemed like forever.

When the door opened, Kaitlyn's dad, Eric, filled the opening. "You made it." He clapped me on the shoulder. "Come on in." He stepped back and let me pass. Once inside, I was assaulted with heavenly smells. The tree was lit, and people were everywhere. The Hughes' house always looked like something out of a movie with every little detail taken care of. Green garland was swagged along the archways, and red candles were burning on various tables. A Nativity was set up along with their nutcracker collection I remember Kaitlyn boasting about when we were younger. Red bows covered anything that would stand still, and soft music filled the air.

I wandered through the house saying hello to people as I passed with one mission on my mind. I needed to find her. I'd spent all day practicing what I'd say when I got here to keep her from leaving, but as my eyes landed on her back I became tongue tied. She looked beautiful standing there with her mother. She was wearing a pair of black slacks and a red sweater. Her mom nodded at me, and Kaitlyn turned and froze. Her mouth opened and closed a few times as her eyes widened at her mother. I watched as she composed herself before coming over to greet me.

"Hi." She smiled. "What are you doing here?"

"Your dad invited me." I held out the wine. "Kinda like old times, huh? Only I was old enough to buy this."

She laughed. "Yeah, I guess."

"Wanna open it?" I shifted on my feet. I'd never been nervous around a woman before, but Kaitlyn put me on edge. I actually cared about her, and after last night I felt like I was walking on cracked ice just praying that I didn't fall through to the icy water below.

"Okay." She turned and led me toward the kitchen. After grabbing a wine key, she took two glasses from the cabinet while I opened the bottle. I poured us each a glass, and then handed her one.

"To us." I clinked my glass with hers and watched her brow furrow.

"There is no us, Eli." She sighed as she leaned against the counter.

"I know. I'm sorry." I grimaced. "That was stupid. I just didn't know what to say. I don't know how I'm supposed to be right now, Kait. I'm trying here."

"I know. I'm sorry too. Let's start over." She smiled before lifting her glass. "To old friends. May we always remember those who mean the most to us and keep the bonds we have with them strong." I clinked my glass to hers and then took a sip.

"I can agree to that." I chuckled as I downed the wine in my glass. I watched Kaitlyn's eyes flare before she hid whatever she was feeling.

We spent the rest of the evening talking about everything we could think of. What we planned to do for New Year's, how the years had changed us, and more about what we'd been doing for the last five years. I could stand there and listen to her talk all night if she'd let me. Kaitlyn always had this way of making anything interesting. It was like she could lure you in, and you'd forget what time it was. Before long, I realized that most of the party guests had left. I glanced around, and that's when I noticed that Kaitlyn's parents were missing.

"They went to bed." She smiled as if she were reading my mind. "It's after midnight. I told them I'd clean up."

"I can help you." I started to stand, but Kaitlyn shook her head.

"You don't need to do that. There's not that much to do. I'm still on Paris time despite trying to acclimate. I'll walk you out."

"Are you telling me I need to leave?" I teased.

"Yeah. I am. I need to go to bed too." She laughed as she pushed at my shoulder. This was the Kaitlyn that I remembered, but this is the one I thought I was dealing with the other night. This woman had me so twisted up I didn't know which way was down at the moment.

"Fine. I can take a hint." I stood and slipped my coat on as Kaitlyn made her way to the door. We stepped out onto the porch, and she wrapped her arms around her middle to ward off the chill. It was then that I realized that I was standing under a small bunch of mistletoe. "Well, what do you know." I pointed up above us.

Kaitlyn's eyes went wide and filled with fear. I'd never seen her look so scared of me before. "That's not a good idea." Her head shook from side to side.

"Why? It's tradition." I stepped closer and wrapped my arm around her, pulling her flush against me. Her body leaned into me, contradicting her words. "You don't want to mess with tradition, do you?"

"It's not that." Her bottom lip quivered as I leaned in.

"Then what is it?" My mouth was so close to hers we were breathing in each other's breath. Every part of me was trying to touch her. I needed to kiss her, and this was the excuse I'd been looking for. We'd had wine and had been laughing together all night. It was perfect until the next two words fell from her lips.

"I'm married," came out in a whisper.

I was hearing things. I had to be. There was no way this woman who I've loved for most of my life was married to another man. "What?" I released her as if touching her hurt me.

"I'm married." She stared at the ground as she stepped back from where I was. "I'm so sorry, Eli." She turned and rushed into the house, leaving me standing there and breaking my heart all over again.

Chapter 5

Present Day

Eli

"Damn it! Sonofa…" I rushed to the sink to stick my hand under the water. You'd think that I'd learned my lesson by now, but I always was a hard head.

"What's wrong?" Jackson's head popped up from around the corner.

"I wasn't paying attention and I touched the crab pot," I grumbled as the cool water ran over my burnt skin. Steam burns were the worst, and lately my head hadn't been in the game. Too much was going on, and I didn't have the heart to tell Jackson that I needed some time off.

"Why don't you let Sam do that?" His brow furrowed. "You've been working nonstop for the last week."

"Maybe I wouldn't have to if someone hadn't gone off and gotten married. Your wife coming in today?" I shot him a look over my shoulder.

"Maybe." He shrugged. "I told her to take her time. She's been real busy lately with redoing the bar menu."

"Whatever," I muttered as I glanced around the kitchen. The last couple of months have been rough for me. Jackson's wife finally started getting some of her memory back. When this happened, my problems seemed small. I put my feelings aside and did what I could to support him. It's what friends do. I've been a mess since last weekend. Kaitlyn called me out of the blue. I sent her to voicemail, but she didn't leave a message. I don't know what she wanted. After she left… again… I swore I wouldn't let her in again.

I still remember that night. Christmas Eve, and all I wanted to do was to kiss her. She dropped the marriage bomb on me, and then disappeared. When I came by the next day to talk through all of it, she was gone. She'd run just like the last time. Her dad had given me some excuse about how she had an emergency at her work, and Henri needed her to come home. I knew it was a lie, but I also knew that I needed to let her go. So that's what I did. I let her go. I deleted her number. I refused to take her calls. I avoided her house. When her parents came into the bar, I made Jackson deal with them. I just couldn't do it again.

I've been doing great with pretending she doesn't exist until this week. It seems like everywhere I go something reminds me of her, and then she started calling. "Is this about HER?"

I turned to see him leaning in the doorway with his arms crossed over his chest. "It doesn't matter."

"I think it does. Maybe you should talk to Tessa. She might be able to help." He pushed off the wood frame and started to walk away before calling over his shoulder, "It couldn't hurt."

What Jackson didn't know, was that he was wrong. It could hurt. I'd suffered so much from that woman breezing in and out of my life that on some days I just wanted to find someone to help me forget. I'd tried to meet someone else, but none of them compared. It was as if I'd put Kaitlyn on this pedestal that no one could ever reach. I didn't even know if the real Kaitlyn could reach it. Some days I wondered if she was even as good as my mind remembered or if it was all a fantasy.

oooooooooo

Kaitlyn

It's been a week. I've been back a week, and it feels like a year. I didn't know what to expect when I came back to Crescent Moon Beach. I guess I thought things would be the same, but I was wrong. This time was different. This time I wasn't leaving, I was here for good. I was going to make this my home.

My parents had helped me find an apartment, and the day after I got home I moved in. I'd been saving money and was working obscene hours to open my own pastry shop. I'd found this old building down the street from Anchor Bay that was for sale. I've been cleaning and painting for the last three days trying to get things ready for an opening next month. I've called Eli every day to try and talk, but he's been ignoring me. I don't even think he knows I'm back. It's been five years since I left for the second time. Five years since I told him about Henri, and I'm beginning to wonder if those five years were too much this time around. I'm not the naïve twenty-three-year-old that came back for Christmas this time around. This time is different. This time I've grown and learned from my mistakes. This time I'm coming home with my eyes open.

I spent most of today painting. I decided that a soft pink and mint green showcased my pastries the best. My dad helped me up until dinner time, then he left. Now, I'm painting by work lights, and hoping that I can finish this last wall before it gets too late. I tried calling Eli again today, but he sent me to voicemail…again. I'm thinking I need to just show up somewhere, only I'm not really dressed to impress.

As the evening turned to night, I finally decided to call it quits. I turned the lights off one by one, placed my brushes in a bucket of water to soak, and grabbed my keys from where they had been tossed on a counter. I was starving, but I needed to go home. I had paint smudged on my cheeks, and a few drops of it in my hair. My jeans had pink and green splattered on them, and there was a giant blob on my shirt. I was a mess.

I opened the front door and stepped out onto sidewalk. I locked up and turned to walk down the street to where I'd parked my car after lunch. When I lifted my head, I almost crashed into him. There standing in front of me was the last person I thought I'd see… Eli. I stumbled back and blinked up at him, "Hey."

"What are you doing here?" His forehead wrinkled as he glanced around like he was looking for someone.

"Following a dream of my own." I smiled before motioning behind me.

Eli glanced around again before turning back to me. "Where's your husband?"

"Paris, last I checked. He decided he liked his girlfriend more than me." It still hurt saying it, but each time it got a little easier. "It's good to see you, Eli."

"Yeah, same." He nodded and I stepped around him to get to my car. "You should come by once I open." I motioned to the glass window in the front of my space "I'll cook for you this time."

"Maybe I will," he smiled. "Hey, Kait."

I turned and watched him.

"It's good seeing you." He waved and then continued on in the direction he was heading.

Sands of Time

I smiled to myself when I reached my car. Maybe this wasn't going to be so bad after all. Maybe, just maybe, things would work out.

Chapter 6

Eli

"It was weird, and painful all at the same time," I muttered as I lifted the beer I was holding to my lips. I'd planned to go home, but after running into Kaitlyn I'd driven straight to Jackson's house instead. "She looked happy. Is it bad that I wish she wasn't? Why can't she be miserable like me?" I shook my head as I stared at the wall of their living room. Jackson and Tessa were cooking dinner, and every once in a while, I'd hear a muffled giggle. It was as if they didn't want me to know that they were happy.

"What did you say to her?" Jackson leaned around the corner and a white flour handprint was visible on his cheek.

"That it was good to see her. I mean, what else should I have said?" I rubbed my face before sighing.

"Maybe that you're pissed," Jackson's sarcastic bark sounded from the kitchen. "You are pissed, right?"

"I don't know what I am anymore," I huffed. "Frustrated, angry, numb? That's it. I'm more numb than anything," I finished off the beer and rose to go get another one.

"Does she know that?" Tessa smiled sweetly as she rounded the corner to place dinner on the table.

"How would she? He rejects her calls every time his phone rings," Jackson rolled his eyes as he waved a fork in my direction. "You should tell her how you feel, Bro," he shrugged and he followed his wife to the table.

"I don't know if now's the best time to do that," Tessa piped up. "He's had a bunch of those." She motioned to my beer as I glanced down at it.

"I'm not drunk," I scoffed as I stood and swayed a little.

"I'm not sure the rest of you knows that," Tessa laughed.

"Well thanks," I shook my head and the room kinda wobbled. Maybe I was a little tipsy.

"You can crash here if you want," Jackson grinned as he served his plate. "We don't mind."

"No thanks. I think I'll walk home," I grabbed my keys and moved toward the door,

"That's three miles, and you haven't eaten," Jackson chuckled.

"I'd walk ten miles if it meant I wasn't sleeping on a couch where I could hear you two fucking each other," I glared at them as Jackson roared with laughter.

"We're not that loud," Tessa giggled. "Well, most of time."

"Suit yourself," Jackson shrugged again before taking a bite of food. He's right. If I was sober I'd realize that walking home was a bad idea. It was dark, I was drunk, and I was angry. Those last two things always made for a night of bad decisions, and it seemed that bad decisions were part of a regular night for me lately.

oooooooo

The section of beach that Jackson and I lived on was fairly rural. The bar was just at the edge of the tourist section, and once you drove passed it you came to a lot of private beach area. I liked it out this way most of the time. Tonight, was not one of those times. It was dark because we didn't have street lights out here, and the grass on the edge of the road was rather tall. I grumbled as I walked along, swinging the beer bottle between my fingers. I'd grabbed one for the road on my way out, and I'd already finished the one I'd been holding. When I twisted the top off, I glanced at the label, and that's when she popped into my head. This particular brand of beer was the kind that Kaitlyn and I were drinking that first night we hung out at the Silver Crane.

"God damn you! Get out of my fucking head," I growled as I lifted the bottle to my lips. It was then that I felt my phone pressing against my ass in my back pocket. I smirked as I reached in and grabbed it. I was being stupid, but I was drunk enough to not care. I pulled up the call history, and there she was. Kaitlyn's number was glowing multiple times where she'd called over the last week. I'd deleted her from my phone but not my mind. I'd had the number memorized for years. I laughed as my finger hovered over it daring me to press down. After a few drunken steps, I lost my balance and pressed it by accident. Guess that was the universe's way of making me call her. I lifted the phone to my ear as it rang on the other end. After a few moments, she picked up.

"Hello?" her voice was groggy and it was then that I realized it was pretty late. "Eli?" I stumbled to a stop and just stared out into the darkness willing myself to talk to her. "I know it's you," she sighed. "Talk to me," her voice quivered and I wondered if she was nervous, or trying not to cry. "I'm glad you called," she pushed forward attempting to fill the dead space.

"What do you want from me?" I growled as my hand gripped the phone tighter. I waited for her to say something, but nothing came. "You keep calling me. You must want something, so what is it?" I stumbling along the side of the road beer in one hand, and phone in the other, waiting for an answer that I wasn't sure I wanted. "Well?" I all but yelled.

I could hear her sniffle before she sighed, "I just want to talk to you." Her voice was almost timid. "Can we meet somewhere for lunch tomorrow, or something?"

"I have to work, remember? I own a bar," I chuckled, but it wasn't funny.

"Why are you acting like this?" a ruffling sound was in the background, and I was guessing she was moving around in bed. Just the idea of her lying there naked made my dick hard. He didn't care that she lied to me. He didn't care that she ran away. He just wanted a warm body.

"Maybe this is me now," I laughed sarcastically. "I mean, you don't even know me anymore."

"That's not true," she whispered.

"Oh yeah? What do you know about me?" I glanced up and realized I'd been standing in the same spot for the last five minutes.

"I know you're hurting, and I'm sorry. I know going home and not talking to you was a mistake. It was a mistake, Eli, and I've been regretting it for the last five years. You don't know me though. You don't know what I've been through, and if you would just listen…" I'd heard enough, and as I shook my head trying to ignore the words that she said, I clicked the phone off. Within a few seconds, it rang again. I didn't have to look at it to know that she was calling me back.

"God damn it!" I roared as I threw the empty bottle that had been hanging in my hand toward the empty lot I was walking passed. Listening to her was like having thousands of tiny razor blades slice across my body. It was painful, and I didn't want to go through it again.

Sands of Time

Knowing that she was back, was killing me, but being near her was so much worse.

I powered my phone down as I reached my driveway, and walked right into my house stopping in kitchen. After grabbing the six pack out of the fridge, and headed out to the beach. I kicked my shoes off, and lowered myself onto the sand. A mix of anger and sadness coursed through me as I cracked open a fresh beer. I don't know what time it was when I finally passed out, but I was finally starting to not care. For the first time in months, Kaitlyn Hughes wouldn't haunt my dreams.

oooooooooo

Kaitlyn

When my alarm went off this morning, I almost rolled over and went back to sleep. I was exhausted from all the work I'd been putting in at my new bakery, and then Eli's late-night phone call didn't help matters. I had only been asleep for a few hours when he called, but after that I spent the wee hours of the morning dissecting everything we said. My emotions were a jumbled mess, and I wasn't sure I'd ever be able to fix them. Eli seemed to want to keep me as an enemy. I couldn't blame him, but deep down I'd kinda hoped that we might be able to be friends one day. I'd never really had that with Henri. We'd gone from a boss/ employee relationship to a husband/wife relationship, at least that's what I'd thought we were.

When I'd returned home from Crescent Moon beach after Christmas five years ago, I'd thought that Henri would be happy to see me. He'd been very supportive of me traveling to see my family. I guess I should have been suspicious. It turns out that he'd been having an affair with one of the interns at the restaurant. All those late-night sessions that he claimed were to help her perfect her methods, were really his chance to screw around on me. I couldn't believe that I'd been so stupid. When I walked in our home after coming from the airport, I'd found separation papers on our dining room table. Henri was sitting on the couch with Gabriella beside him. With a stoic expression, he told me he loved her and wanted out. I'd stuck around for the next four years trying to find the excitement and happiness that I'd once had working in Paris, but it just wasn't the same. I yearned for the comforts of home, and having my family to support me emotionally. Last month, I'd packed up my things and moved home, never looking back until now. I don't think I was every truly happy with Henri. I think I'd been fooling myself, but Eli didn't know that. All he knew was I'd kept my marriage from him, and left without even saying good bye.

oooooooooo

After showering and throwing on my painting clothes, I grabbed a granola off the counter and headed back to my bakery. Pulling up in front of the building had me feeling pride for the first time in a long time. I had something that was mine. I'd bought it on my own, and I was going to make it a success on my own. I hopped out of my car and jogged up the steps. After unlocking the door, I stepped inside and gathered my brushes. I'd finished most of the painting already, it was the details that I still needed to work on. My display coolers were being delivered today, and if everything went well I'd be opening up in another week or so.

I climbed up on my ladder, and began taping my stencils to the wall. I'd picked an intricate design for my lettering, and had decided last night to wait until morning to attempt it. Blissful Bites was my baby, and every detail mattered down to gold sparkles that glittered in the sunlight.

The walls were a mint green and pink, so I used a darker version of that for the accents. I had two giant chalkboards hanging behind what would be the counter, and a few small tables scattered about. I wanted my customers to be able to sit and talk if they wanted to eat their treats right away. I planned to have several staple items, but then change the others as the seasons changed. Pumpkin Spice was big in the fall, but lemon was more of a demand in the summer. I had area all planned out for cake tasting too. I'd hoped that once people started trying my cakes, I'd be able to bake for some brides. As much as I loved making specialty items like my Christmas tarts, I loved the challenge of a multi-tiered wedding cake.

It didn't take as long as I'd thought it would to get the lettering finished, and before I knew it I was standing in the center of a fully painted room. I smiled as I looked around at what I'd accomplished. It was all starting to come together, and I'd done it all by myself. Henri had lit a fire in me when he'd pushed me to the side, and the harder I worked, the brighter it burned. I'd all but forgotten the delivery I was waiting on until the bell over the door sounded. "You can bring them right in," I called without looking behind me.

"Bring what in," a voice I didn't think I'd hear anytime soon startled me. I spun around to find a pair of crystal blue eyes staring back, but the anger I thought I'd find in them was missing. The only thing there was sadness, sadness I'd put there. "Can we talk?" he stuffed his hands in his shorts pockets and leaned against the doorway just watching me.

Chapter 7

Kaitlyn

I stepped backwards, stumbling slightly. "Sure." I waved with my arm signally Eli to come in. His head bent down as he started to move forward, his shoulder brushing mine as he passed me.

"I'm sorry about last night," he turned to face me. His eyes were red, and he looked exhausted.

"It's fine," I gave him a half smile. I wasn't sure what to make of the entire situation, so I was afraid to push him too far.

"No it's not," his hands burrowed back into pockets. "I was an ass last night. I've been an ass a lot lately."

"You have your reasons," I laughed lightly, and he cracked a smile for the first time in a long time.

"The place looks great," he spun around taking in the bakery.

"Thanks. I like to think that I'm doing ok," I began pacing because I knew if I stood still I might try to hug him, and that would not be good. Whatever truce we'd settled on here was still very fresh, and I didn't want to do anything to disrupt that.

"It's better than ok, Kait. It looks… wow!" he began moving too, dragging his fingers lightly along the counter tops. "Do you need any help?"

"The delivery guy should be here soon with my coolers, but other than that it's just little things like cleaning and stocking that are left to do," I smiled.

"When do you plan to open?" he crossed his arms over his chest.

"Monday, I think," I laughed. I didn't sound very sure of myself, but that may have been partly Eli's fault. No matter our relationship at the moment, he still made me nervous. Being around him made me feel like that same seventeen-year-old that was in love with him all those years ago.

"When do you plan to start the baking?" he moved closer and my stomach did a little flip.

"Sunday," I swallowed. "I've still got to hire a few more staff, and I need a baker that can help out when we're extra busy."

"I can help you if you want," he stepped closer, and I stepped back.

"Why?" I was confused. What did all this mean. Last night he hated me, and this morning he wants to help. "What is all this?"

Eli let out a deep breath. "I'm trying to be an adult, and help you. We used to make a great team. I'd like to think that we could bake side by side and be a good team again."

"Don't you have a bar to cook for?" I cocked my head to the side.

"Eh," he shrugged. "I can step away after the dinner rush. They'll be ok by then, and last I checked" he moved closer "you were a night owl."

"I still am," I could feel my face heating, and I looked away.

"Ok," he nodded and turned for the door. "See you Sunday night, Kait," he waved as he stepped out onto the street. I could hear muffled voices through the windows, and when I looked out I saw the truck parked on the curb and several men unloading my coolers. I couldn't help but do a little jump as the excitement of all this coming together coursed through me.

ooooooooo

Eli

I was an idiot, plain and simple. As I climbed into my car to head to the bar, I began talking to myself. "What do you plan to accomplish by helping her? Don't you think it's going to be painful being stuck in a kitchen alone with her for who knows how long? You're an idiot, Eli, and she's going to shatter you again." I grumbled as the voice in my head told me I was stupid, but my heart didn't care. It still loved her, and I think she could probably do anything to me and I'd still come back.

When I reached Anchor Bay, I parked, and made my way to the kitchen. Jackson was in his office balancing the books, and Tessa was behind the bar getting things ready for the night. Sam was working at the prep table when I rounded the corner. "They shorted us on clams again, Boss," he grumbled.

"Fucking great," I growled before turning around, and storming off toward Jackson's office. I stomped through door and slammed it shut just as his head popped up.

"I don't know what you've got up your ass this morning, but I'm not in the mood," his voice was tight as he stared at me.

"I think it's time we break up with our fish supplier," I shook my head. "I know you like him, Bro, but he's fucked me over again."

"What happened?" Jackson closed his laptop and rocked back in his chair.

"We're short on our clam order. Last week we only got half the lobsters, the week before," I rolled my eyes as I tossed my hands in the air "who the fuck knows, but I'm sure it was something. I can't make clam chowder without clams."

"Red tide is happening now. Did you check to see if that's why?" Jackson gave me that all knowing look that said I was over reacting.

"It doesn't matter. How does that explain the lobster problem?" I huffed as I started to pace.

"Fine," Jackson held his hands up in surrender. "I'll call Joe and see what he says. If we can't get the order by tonight, then we'll start shopping around. Did you call Kaitlyn?" my head whipped around and I stumbled to a stop.

"What does that have to do with anything?" I said a little too loudly.

"You've been flipping out for days, and it seems you've reached a breaking point. You need to talk to her, and sort all this out," he smirked as he lifted his hands to rest them behind his head.

"Why don't you stay out of it?" I warned.

"Oh," he laughed "kinda like you stayed out of it when Tessa and I were circling each other?"

"Jacks," I warned again.

"It's obvious there's something there. You wouldn't be this wound up if there wasn't. You need to explore that," he mused.

"I don't think I can," I closed my eyes and pinched the bridge of my nose.

"Sure, you can. Have a drink, or ten, and go over to her place," he snickered.

"Real classy," I muttered.

"Hey," he shrugged "if it doesn't work you can blame it on the booze."

"I'm going back to the kitchen. Fix the clam issue," I jabbed my finger in the air at him before rounding the corner and almost running into Tessa. "Tell your husband to stop trying to fix me."

"He's stubborn. It would be a waste of time," she giggled before stepping around me and into his office. The clicked shut, and I knew it would be at least fifteen minutes before either of them emerged. Was Jackson, right? Did I just need to get over myself, and make a move? Would Kaitlyn even want that?

oooooooo

The last couple of days have been a blur, but when the dinner rush began to die down on Sunday night, I got that nervous feeling of a first date all over again. I hadn't talked to Kaitlyn since I promised to help, but I planned to make good on my offer. I'd made up a bullshit excuse of needing an early night for a date, and Jackson agreed. He'd said something along the lines of me needing to get laid before I burned the place down.

I told myself a thousand times throughout the night that I was an idiot, but when ten o'clock rolled around, I removed my apron and headed for my car. The drive to the bakery was short. It was right down the road, but when I pulled up I wondered if she was even there. It was dark, and no lights appeared to be on in the kitchen. I climbed out and jogged over to the door. A quick pull on the handle reaffirmed my previous thoughts. The door was locked, and I couldn't see any movement as I cupped my eyes to the glass. Deciding to be a creeper, I began walking around the building looking for signs of life. When I reached the back door, it was propped open, and I could hear singing. I laughed as Kaitlyn's offkey voice filtered through the air. She had to be alone because I've never known her to sing in front of anyone.

I made my way through the dark listening to her sing until I came to a light that was glowing from what had to be the kitchen. I paused in the tiny hallway, and just watched. She was standing behind a large metal counter swaying her hips as she stirred something in a big metal bowl. Her hair was pulled up with a pink bandana tied around it. A few stray pieces were hanging around her face, and the black t-shirt she was wearing clung to her. My eyes trailed farther down and I about swallowed my tongue. She was wearing what had to be the shortest shorts I'd ever seen. The denim was worn and there were tears leaving a fringed effect.

I shifted in the shadows and that's when the damn floor gave me away. The board beneath me squeaked, and Kaitlyn spun around dropping the bowl she was holding and screaming at the same time.

"It's me!" I rushed into the room. "It's just me," I held my hands out in defense as she looked like she was ready to take a swing at me.

"Fuck Eli!" she screamed. "Why the hell are you spying on me?"

I sighed as I rolled my eyes. "I wasn't spying on you. I just got here. I said I'd help. Remember?"

"Sure," she shook her head. "Help," she muttered under her breath. "The one time he actually does what he says he's going to do, and I look like this," she shook her head again as she squatted down and began picking up the mess she made. I don't think she intended for me to hear the last part, but I couldn't help it.

"If you don't want the help, I can leave," I chuckled.

"Nah," she laughed. "You can stay," she blew a piece of hair out of her face as she stood to go grab a broom. It was then that I saw the black shirt was covered in flour.

"You got a little something…" I motioned to her chest.

"Un huh," she rolled her eyes as she shoved me out of her way. "How about you start that sweet bread recipe again? It's on the counter."

Sands of Time

I stepped over the wet spot on the floor and started gathering ingredients as she put the broom and dust pan away. When she came back, she sidled up right next to me. I pushed everything between us, and she started flipping through her book for a cookie recipe. We mixed, cut, rolled, and punched dough like partners that had been working together their entire life. It had been years since we'd done this, and I was amazed that we still could do it without talking to one another. Hours passed, and tray after tray was pulled from the oven. The display cases in the front of the bakery began to fill, and time seemed to fly by.

"Shit!" Kaitlyn sighed as she leaned against the counter. "I need to go to bed."

"What time is it?" I glanced around looking for a clock.

"Four am," she yawned and dried the last pan. "I guess I should have started earlier.

"Four?!" I almost whimpered. "Jackson's gonna kill me."

"Why?" she looked confused.

"I'm gonna have to call in. I usually do the prep work, and tomorrow is lobster day. Our truck arrives at five. I need to sleep or I'll be shit for the dinner shift," I rubbed my palms down my face.

"I'm sorry," Kaitlyn bit her lip. "I appreciate the help, but you didn't need to stay so late."

"Nonsense," I laughed. "It was kinda fun."

"Kinda?" she smiled and it seemed almost like flirting. "I was having fun until I did this," she motioned to the white powder that still clung to her top.

"Nothing a shower won't fix," I winked.

"Oh god. A hot shower sounds so good right now," she closed her eyes and the way her voice quieted did something to me.

Before I could stop myself, my feet began moving toward her. I stopped right behind her, and placed my hands on her shoulders and began kneading them. She groaned, her head falling forward. My feet shuffled closer to her causing my entire body to press against her back. My dick twitched where her ass was cradled against me. I leaned down putting my mouth right by her ear. "There are a lot of things that sound good right now, but a shower alone isn't one of them," the words slipped from my lips and she froze.

"What are you saying," she murmured, her voice full of confusion.

"Fuck! I don't know," I released her and stepped back. "I'm sorry. I shouldn't have done that. I need to go," I spun towards the door, and rushed away as quickly as my feet would allow. I needed to get away from her. Being near her made me stupid, and stupid Eli is the one that always gets hurt. I needed space, and air, and I needed them without her.

Chapter 8

Kaitlyn

When my alarm went off this morning, I almost turned it off and went back to sleep. It was just when my eyes closed that my brain caught up and reminded me that today was the day. I was finally at the point of making one of my dreams come true. I rubbed the sleep out of my eyes as I sat up, and smiled at my tired reflection. With energy I didn't think I had, I dressed and went to my kitchen for my coffee. It didn't take long for me to start walking to the bakery with my travel mug in hand. I loved living close by. It gave me the chance to go home, but if something happened I could always come back.

When I rounded the corner to Blissful Bites, there was already a line forming at the door. I clapped my hands giddily as I turned to head to the back of the building. The two girls I hired yesterday to help run the counter were waiting for me, and greeted me with anxious smiles. "Morning Brenna. Morning Chloe," I waved.

"Morning Boss. Looks like a good crowd out there," they both motioned toward the street.

"Let's hope so," I unlocked the back door, and we all filed in. "I need to get the pastry cream out of the cooler. Why don't you two start turning on lights and load the cash drawer?"

"Sure thing," Brenna began flipping switches as I went toward the walk-in. I was planning to sell cannoli's, but you have to fill them when they're ordered or they get soggy. When I came back with the bag of pastry cream, both girls were smiling behind the counter. "You ready for this?" I started walking toward the door. They both nodded, and I flipped the lock and propped the door open.

It was warm out, but there was a nice breeze today. I wanted to keep the door open as much as I could. I loved the way the air smelled at the beach, and I missed so much of this living in Paris.

oooooooooo

Eli

Sands of Time

I awoke to my phone vibrating on my night table. I had seven missed calls when I checked it last, but I'd gone back to sleep. Jackson had told me he'd be fine, and I wasn't going to give him a chance to change his mind. I didn't even check the time when I answered.

"What?" I barked into the phone. I was still exhausted from helping Kaitlyn, and not in the mood for his antics.

"Do you plan to work the dinner shift today?" Jackson sounded slightly aggravated. "I mean, I guess I can the run the whole place if you can't make it."

"I said I'd be in at noon. That's plenty of time to get ready for dinner," I grumbled as I rolled to my back and tossed one arm over my head.

"It is plenty of time, but it's three o'clock dude," now he sounded annoyed.

"Yeah right," I muttered as I turned my head to look at my alarm clock. Shit! It was three. "I'm sorry. Give me a half hour. I'm coming right now," I clicked the phone off, and rushed to get dressed. I knew I could probably get there faster, but I didn't want to promise him something and then be late again.

I grabbed a pair of dark jeans off the end of my bed, and sniffed them. They didn't stink, so I slipped them on, and then grabbed a clean t-shirt from a drawer. I was going to be in the kitchen tonight, so I didn't need my 'owner' attire. I slipped on a baseball hat, brushed my teeth, and then grabbed my kitchen shoes. On the way out the door, I shoved my phone into my pocket, and then almost ran to my car. The fact that I hadn't eaten or even had a cup of coffee, slipped my mind as I rushed across town to the bar.

When I drove passed Blissful Bites, there was a line at the door. I knew Kaitlyn would be a success. She always was a good cook, and now she had the training and experience to back it up. When I pulled into the parking lot of Anchor Bay, I took a few deep breaths, before climbing out, and rushing in.

"I know, I know," I sighed and waved at Jackson when he came around the corner.

"Please tell me that last night's date actually ended happy, and that's why you're late," he began to follow me to the kitchen.

"Not exactly, and that's all you're getting," I waved him off as I tied an apron around my waist.

"Whatever," he shook his head. "Let me know what you think of these lobsters, and take a look at the crab in the cooler. I used a different supplier this time. If we like him, we can sign a deal with him starting next week."

"Will do. Now get out of my kitchen," I laughed as he turned to leave.

oooooooooo

The night went better than I thought it would, with only a handful of hiccups. The new seafood Jackson had ordered was well above the grade of what we've been serving, and I was actually able to make a bisque to put on special tonight. The kitchen ran like a well-oiled machine, and when things finally started to slow down, my exhaustion began to catch up.

"I can manage if you want to take a breathier, boss," Sam, my sous chef, called from where he was plating a few dishes.

"Thanks Sam," I sighed as I stepped away from the stove. Business usually got quiet now with only a few food orders here and there, and then the kitchen would close leaving the bar to carry the business. "I'll see you in the morning for prep." I waved, and then tossed my apron in the basket before heading into the office. Jackson was usually closing out receipts at this point, but things had been running differently since he and Tessa hooked up.

Sure enough, when I rounded the corner, I could see him leaning against the bar. He was talking to one of our regulars while Tessa pulled the second drawer. She was down to two bartenders, and they could work off one well. I decided against my better judgement to go say hi. Normally I wouldn't think twice, but looking down at myself told me I shouldn't be in the dining room. My jeans had food splattered on them, and I'd sweat so much that my t-shirt was plastered to my chest. Jackson spotted me though, and motioned for me to come over.

"Hey Phil," I waved as I stepped out of the shadows.

"Hey Eli. Busy tonight, huh?" he smiled as he lifted his beer.

"End of summer always brings a crowd. All the tourists are trying to get that last little bit of summer in before school starts back up," I took off my hat, ran my fingers through my sweaty hair, and then replaced it.

"Man you stink," Jackson teased as he leaned closer. His voice lowered as he mumbled, "Phil wasn't why I called you up here. You have a visitor. She asked to see you," he nodded toward the other end of the bar, and without even looking I knew exactly who it was. "You finally talk to her?" he snickered.

"None of ya," I grumbled back as I turned and confirmed my suspicions. There, sitting on the corner stool was Kaitlyn nursing a beer. Our eyes met, and she smiled. "I'm done for the night," I muttered as I slapped Jackson's shoulder.

"Sure Bro. I'll close up," he grumbled sarcastically.

"You owe me for all the crap I covered for you when that one fucked your head up," I hissed as I began striding toward Kaitlyn. "Hey," I waved.

"I hope this is ok," she spun the bottle between her fingers. "We closed up, and I didn't really want to go home."

"It's fine. How did it go today?" I stepped behind the bar so I could face her despite the dirty look I got from Tessa.

Kaitlyn grinned so big I thought her face might cramp, "We sold out of everything except the pies. Most people don't buy a whole pie, so I expected that," she shrugged as she giggled. "I can't thank you enough for last night. Let me get you a drink."

"I drink for free here, remember," I laughed.

"Right," she nodded in embarrassment. "Sorry."

"It's ok," I shrugged again. "A beer does sound nice. Maybe we can get one tomorrow? I get out at nine."

"Are you asking me out?" she teased.

"No. I'm asking if you want to get a drink somewhere," I flirted. I don't know where this was coming from, but she was back and for some reason I couldn't seem to stay away.

"Sure. How about my place? I'll cook for you," she nibbled her lip as she started peeling the label off her bottle.

"It's a date," I chuckled.

"Wait!" her brow furrowed. "I thought you said... never mind."

I knew I needed space, but I also knew that sitting here and talking to her made me feel something I hadn't in a long time. Dare I say it was happiness? "I'll be right back," I held my hand up as I rounded the bar and rushed toward the kitchen.

I quickly ladled a cup of the lobster bisque that I'd made tonight, and grabbed some crackers. As I carried it toward the bar, I began to second guess myself. If she'd wanted food, she would have ordered some. "Here," I set it in front of her, and grabbed some flatware from under the bar.

"This smells amazing," she hummed as she blew on a spoonful before slipping it into her mouth. "Oh my god! Eli!"

"That was tonight's special," I grinned. I was proud of myself, and the look on her face said she was too.

"You made this?" she had a tiny bit of doubt there, but squashed it.

"I can cook more than desserts," I laughed. "I taught most of the staff the recipes we use."

"You'll have to teach me this one," she spooned another bite in.

"That can be arranged," I reached over and put my hand on top of hers. She flinched slightly, but didn't remove it. Her eyes darted down though, and she just stared as I gave it a gentle squeeze.

The air was thick, and the sounds of the bar faded away as my blood seemed to heat even more. Kaitlyn finished her beer along with the bisque. She shifted on her stool like she was uncomfortable before finally giving in.

"I really need to get home. It's going to be an early morning tomorrow to get everything restocked and I need sleep tonight." She slowly pulled her hand out from under mine, and grimaced. I felt it too, the loss. I wanted to hold her hand again. I wanted to kiss her again. I wanted everything again… no matter how bad it might hurt in the end. Kaitlyn was back, and I was done resisting her.

Chapter 9

Kaitlyn

What the hell was I thinking? My mouth decided to have a mind of its own when it invited him over here. Now, I'm pacing my kitchen trying to decide what to cook for dinner. Eli and I haven't talked much over the last couple of days, and I'm now seeing that that was probably a good thing. I thought things would be better if we could be friends. I never thought we'd ever be more than that. I mean, he hated me for leaving him all those years ago. I stoked that fire even more when I came back, and then dropped the marriage bomb on him. When we ran into each other last month, I figured I'd be lucky if he ever talked to me again.

We're so far past that now, but I don't know what we are. Are we friends? Are we more? Less? What does he want from me? All those unanswered calls make no sense after the way he was flirting at the bar. Was he even flirting? I blew out at breath as I yanked open my refrigerator and grabbed a bottle of wine. I needed alcohol for this. I was going to drive myself mad with the "what ifs" today. I needed to cook. Cooking always helped, and now was my chance to impress him with my skills. Yes, I was a pastry chef, but I could also cook other things.

I grabbed my recipe book from my book shelf. It was a combination of things I'd made or tried, and things I wanted to try. I scrapped the idea of anything to do with seafood since Eli cooked that every day. I know I don't eat sweets very much anymore because I bake them every day. I can't imagine him choosing a seafood dish on a night that he's away from the bar.

As I flipped the pages, I kept coming back to the lamb chops. I'd made them before, and there were little notes jotted down and ways I wanted to tweak the recipe. Deciding that this was it, I made my grocery list, and grabbed my purse. I felt guilty taking the day off from the bakery, but I'd learned early on that you have to a break for yourself. I'd managed to hire several staff members, and after stopping in this morning I realized that Blissful Bites was in good hands.

I laughed to myself as I pulled into the parking lot of the store. This was where it all happened five years ago. I'd come to pick up a few things for my parents, and Eli had practically run me over in the meat department. I wondered if he ever thought about it when he came shopping. I meandered happily around the store grabbing the items I needed before going next door to get the cognac for the sauce. If anything, I could calm my nerves with a few sips of that.

When I got home, I went to work preparing our dinner. Eli had texted me around lunch time and said that he might be able to get out early. They were overstaffed, and a couple of his cooks wanted extra hours. Rather than send them home, he was going to leave. He failed to mention what time that would be but I found out soon enough. As I was stirring the cream sauce for the lamb, there was a knock at the door.

"Just a sec!" I yelled as I wiped my hands on a towel. I checked the lamb again before heading to my door. I was renting a small two-bedroom house about two blocks from the bakery. When I pulled open the door, there he was grinning at me. "Hey," I smiled as I stepped back to let him in.

ooooooooo

Eli

She stood there blushing as she motioned for me to come inside. I'd grabbed a bottle of wine on the way because showing up at a woman's house empty handed was something only a tool would do, and that just wasn't me. "Thanks," I nodded as I stepped by her. She closed the door, and then breezed passed me towards the kitchen.

"Would you like something to drink? Dinner will be ready shortly. I wasn't sure when you'd be here. It's such a nice a day. I thought we could eat on the patio." I followed the direction she'd gone, and just when I rounded the corner, she spun and crashed into my chest.

I grabbed her shoulders to steady her. "Relax," I breathed out next to her ear. I pulled back and made eye contact. She blinked a few times, and then stepped back breaking the contact. "I'm fine, and outside sounds great." I tried to help out, break the tension.

"How about you open that?" she handed me a wine key and pointed to the bottle I'd set on the counter. "I'm gonna check this one last time, and then we can eat."

I carefully uncorked the wine, and poured us each a glass as Kaitlyn pulled a pan from the oven. "That smells delicious," I sighed. I hadn't eaten lunch today, and my stomach growled in protest.

"Thanks. I haven't made this in years. I hope you like lamb," she smiled as she set the pan on top of the stove, and began serving our plates. I watched in fascination as she used sauces and garnishes to position the lamb and what looked like julienne vegetables so elegantly. "This way," she nodded as she turned towards a glass door.

I followed her with the bottle of wine and our glasses. When we stepped outside, we were enclosed in what looked like a small courtyard. There were trellises that formed a small square around the table. Despite the fact that fall was just around the corner, it was still warm out and the flowers still lush and fragrant. A few torches and candles were placed sporadically around the area, and red linens covered the rod iron table and chairs set.

"I feel like I'm in a restaurant," I chuckled as I set the wine on the table, and attempted to pull out Kaitlyn's chair.

She smiled as she set the plates in front of us. "I had a small balcony off of my flat when I lived in Paris. It wasn't nearly as nice as this, but I loved eating outside. Unfortunately, I usually ate alone because Henri was working.

I went silent at her comment about her husband. She hadn't divulged much about him in all our encounters, and I didn't want argue tonight. I'd be lying though if I said it didn't sting a little when she mentioned him. "Sorry," she grimaced.

"It's ok," I lowered myself into my chair but didn't move to start eating.

"No, it's not," she folded her napkin in her lap.

"Do you want to talk about him?" I mirrored her movements. "It's ok if you do." I was lying through my teeth now. I didn't want to talk about him. I didn't want to think about the fact that she chose him over me, or that he'd been the one touching her for all those years. All the things we talked about doing together when we were kids... he did them with her instead of me.

"I," she twisted the napkin in her lap. "I don't know. I feel like you deserve to know, but that's not what this dinner is about."

"He really messed you up, huh?" I mused as I watched her take a bit of her lamb. Her eyes closed and she hummed in satisfaction as she relaxed back into her chair. "I guess that means it's good," I laughed.

"So good," she mumbled around the bite she was chewing.

"How did you meet Henri?" I tossed an easy question out there. As much as I knew this conversation was going to hurt, I also knew it needed to happen.

Kaitlyn's cheeks turned red, "He was my boss."

"And?" I pressed.

"And what?" she took another bite. "Do you really want to know all of this?"

I swallowed and took a sip of wine, "Yes, I do."

"I met Henri when I was in culinary school. His restaurant was where I interned my last year. I worked with his sous chef. When I graduated, he hired me full time. It was then that things began to get serious. I mean, there were moments before that when he tried to escalate things between us, but I always pulled back. He was my boss. I thought it was wrong," she shrugged as she lifted her glass. I watched as she put it to her lips and quickly polished off what was in there. I watched in somewhat amusement as she grabbed the bottle and refilled the glass. I didn't say anything, because I thought I might get the real story now that she seemed to be relaxing a little.

"The day I reported to work as an employee and not a student was the first time he kissed me." Her face contorted in disgust and what appeared to be anger. "He was smooth. He said all the right things, and made me feel special. I was holding back though, and he knew it. He waited for me to be ready, and meanwhile taught me everything he knew. We were a team, and spent most of every day together. If we weren't working in the restaurant, he was teaching me a new technique. I was completely blind to what was happening." She downed another glass of wine, her plate abandoned as she stared off into the distance. I could tell her thoughts were in Paris, and her past was running like a movie through her mind. I did this daily after she left, looking for where I made my mistakes, the little things that I thought I didn't pick up on. I knew what was happening, but I couldn't stop it. A sick part of me needed to know this. I needed to know that if I went after what I wanted, there wouldn't be a ghost standing in the shadows to take her away again.

"We got married after six months. Six months!" She slammed her fist on the table. "I thought we were in love. Every time I mentioned coming home to visit, he found a reason for me to stay," she rolled her eyes. "I was stupid enough to believe that he loved me, that he wanted me near him, but I think it was his way of controlling me. All the little things that I would mention about here… he always found some way to bring them to our home. He didn't want kids, I did. Now here I am alone." Another glass of wine went down, and she laughed as she poured the last little bit into her glass. "I hope you didn't want this?" she giggled as she swayed slightly. "I have more inside."

"I think you need to eat," I eyed her almost full plate.

"Yeah, maybe," she scooped another bite into her mouth and then continued her rant.

"I thought it was weird that he wanted me to come home five years ago. I mean, it was always a problem in the past, but I had my suspicions that something was up so I came. I came with the plan to stay."

My head whipped back at that. "What?"

"I know right? I was going to stay, and then you came along and messed up my head," she glared at me. "You showed up at my house. You made me remember. You made me feel!" She hit the table again.

"Kait," I reached over and tried to touch her arm.

"No! Don't touch me right now," a small tear began making its way down her cheek. "I went back home knowing I could never come here again. I wasn't the woman who cheated on her husband. I wouldn't be her no matter how much I wanted to. I went back with the mindset that I would tell Henri how I felt and we would make things work. He would make me remember why I married him in the first place."

"Kait. You don't need to do this," I slid my chair toward her.

"I came home early and unexpected. I came home to separation papers and my husband with the newest intern." She looked at me now, her eyes full of tears and her lip quivering. "I came home to the realization that it wasn't me he wanted, he just wanted the interns and when we married, that had been me. I'd been the latest intern. When I became the employee, he saw no use for me."

"I'm so sorry," I grabbed her hand and squeezed it.

"I came back here to do what I always said I would do. I came back to start over. I came back to prove that I didn't need Henri Jauffret to be successful. I could do this on my own."

"You're right. You don't need him," I turned her chair to face me. "You don't need anyone to make that bakery successful. You're a brilliant chef, Kait. I'll be the first to admit that."

"I know, but thanks for saying it. I needed to hear that," she wiped at her eyes as she turned toward our half eaten dinner. "You haven't eaten much. Don't you like it?"

"It's great, but you're more important to me right now," my stomach growled in protest.

"I think your stomach disagrees," she laughed as she cut a bite, and fed it to me.

"Mmmm," I groaned as I chewed the tender lamb. She cut another bit and quickly put it to my lips. "I think it might taste better this way," I teased.

"Maybe," she flirted back.

"I'll prove it," I cut a piece, and this time, fed it to her.

Her eyes fell closed as she slowly chewed. "You might be onto something."

"I know I am." We went back and forth like this until we finished, and she reached for her glass.

"I'm all out," she pouted as she stared at the empty glass. "Can I have yours," she smiled coyly up at me as she leaned closer.

"Why don't we move this over there where it'll be more comfortable, and I'll consider it," I nodded to the settee in the corner.

Without saying a word, Kaitlyn rose and began shuffling to the corner of her patio. When I sat down with my glass, she snuggled right up next to me. Every part of me told me to slow down. She was on the verge of drunk, and she'd just poured her heart out. Her nerves were raw, but my body didn't care. All it saw was the girl I've loved since I was sixteen. It saw life dangling her in front of me, and daring me to make a move. I've put space between us, trying to be friends, but my heart doesn't want a friend right now. My heart wants a partner, a person who knows me inside and out, and that person is Kaitlyn.

"Now, give me the wine," she giggled as she reached for it.

"I said share," I lifted it out of her reach. When she stuck out her lip in a pout, I made my move. I quickly took a sip, and then leaned it. My hand slipped around her jaw, and cradled the back of her head. "Tastes pretty good," I murmured as I leaned closer and pressed my lips to hers.

Chapter 10

Kaitlyn

This kiss had been five years in the making, and a part of me had been waiting for this moment all night. His lips tasted like the wine we'd been drinking, and I let him devour me willingly. My mouth parted, inviting him in and he took full advantage. His head tipped to the side, his tongue sweeping passed my lips, and dueling with my own. I'd long forgotten why I'd resisted, and lifted my arms to wrap around his neck.

He pulled back panting, and placed a light peck on the corner of my mouth, "What are we doing, Kait?"

"I don't know, but I like it," I half whispered half giggled. "Do you we really have to dissect it tonight?" I stuck my lip out in a pout as I leaned in.

I could see the conflict in his eyes, but when I connected our mouths again, he groaned and picked up right where he'd left off. "You're like a drug, Kait. I can't resist you."

He panted as he lifted my hips, and placed me on his lap. One leg was folded beside us, the other hanging off the settee, I used my hands for leverage on his shoulders as I rolled my hips. It had been a year since Henri and I had been together, and my body was slowly remembering what Eli had felt like all those years ago. We were kids then, so I can only imagine what time and experience has done for him.

"Whoa," his hands went to my hips to still me. "Slow down, Kait." He pulled away, and the rejection stung.

"Why?" I gasped as my eyes darted around his face. "Don't you want me?"

"You're drunk and hurt, and I don't want to be some revenge fuck for you," he released my hips, and reached for where my hands were still gripping his shoulders. "I can't believe I'm saying this, but I think we need to stop." I scrambled off his lap, and almost fell as I moved to get away from him.

The nights of rejection from Henri surged to the forefront of my mind as I sat there stewing. Eli couldn't possibly understand, but I didn't care. I was angry, and even though he was doing the right thing, I didn't care. "You need to leave," my voice was low, threatening.

"Stop," he begged as he looked forlornly into my eyes.

"Please leave," I repeated through a clenched jaw.

"Listen to me, Kait," he turned toward me, and used both hands to cradle my jaw. "I want you. There's no mistaking that. It's killing me to turn you down tonight, but" he swallowed "when we do this, I want you sober. I don't want you to have any regrets, no walls up. I want it to be about us when we make love, not your ex-husband. I don't want him to even enter your mind when I'm sinking between your thighs. Do you hear me?"

I closed my eyes and sighed. He was right. I knew it, and he knew it, but it still hurt. I nodded.

"Good. Why don't you let me help you to bed, and I'll clean this up," he motioned to the table with our dinner dishes still sitting on it.

"You don't have to," I feebly replied.

"I know," he kissed the tip of my nose and stood offering his hand. "Come on," he gave it a gentle tug, and I followed him inside. "Which way to your room?" he glanced around, and I pointed to the right.

"End of the hall," I yawned, and it was then that I realized that my lack of sleep this week was finally catching up with me. He led me into my room, pulled back the covers, removed my shoes and jeans, and tucked me in.

"Sweet dreams, Kait," he smiled softly before pressing a kiss to my forehead, and then he turned and left. As my eyes drifted closed, I could hear him moving around my house but I was too tired to care.

oooooooooo

Eli

I made the right decision. I told myself this over and over again as I brought our dishes and the table linens in from the patio all the while dealing with a bad case of blue balls. It could have been so easy for me to let her keep going, to let her ease that ache that we both had. I knew better though. I knew that if I wanted this second chance to work, I needed to go slow no matter how much it hurt, literally.

I carefully loaded the dishes into the dishwasher, wiped down the counters, and hand washed the pots and pans. I knew how particular I was about my kitchen so I could only imagine how Kaitlyn was about hers. Once the last dish was put away, I crept down the hall like some sort of stalker to check on her. I pushed her door open a crack, and almost swallowed my tongue. She was lying on her stomach in the middle of the bed with the covers pooled around her waist. One bare leg was sticking out to the side, and her bare back was on full display. At some point after I'd left her, she'd managed to strip apparently.

My fingers curled into my palms as I resisted going in there and touching her. She shifted in her sleep, and I sprung back, worried that she'd catch me watching her, or worse, I'd get a glimpse of what the front side of her looked like. I'd never be able to keep my hands off of her if I saw that. "Fuck, fuck, fuck!" I hissed as I moved quickly down the hallway. "Need to leave. Go home Eli. Go home before you do something stupid," I growled to myself, but the thing was, I couldn't. I couldn't leave, and I don't know why. Being this close to her was torture, but in some sick way I liked it. I felt alive for the first time in months, and I didn't want to lose that.

I somehow convinced myself that I needed to be close by for whatever reason. I'd striped out of my shirt and pants, and curled up on Kaitlyn's couch. There was a throw over the back of it, so I pulled that down to cover myself, and now I'm staring at the ceiling wide away. I was tired about five minutes ago, but now I feel like I could run a marathon or something. Every creak the house makes, every time the waves crash, my eyes fly open as if something is watching me. It's almost as if I feel like Kaitlyn is going to catch me sleeping over. Part of me knows I shouldn't be doing this, but another part of me can't leave her. She's finally let me in, and now I want it all.

I'd just closed my eyes for the hundredth time when my phone buzzed. I rubbed my eyes and looked at the clock. It was only two a.m., but it felt later. Of course, when I swiped the screen, Jackson's name would pop up.

Jackson: Stopped by with beers tonight. Where are you?

Eli: Told you. Dinner with Kait.

Jackson: Still? How many courses did she cook?

Eli: 1. She's asleep.

Jackson: And you are?

Eli: Not. What do you want?

I laid there waiting for the three little dots to appear again, but instead my phone started vibrating in my hand. I clicked the accept button, and before I could even say hello, Jackson started in on me, "Are you at her place now?"

"What are you, fifteen?" I grumbled. "And if you thought that, why the fuck would you call me?"

"Definitely not at her place if you're aggravated. No, nookie for you, huh?" he snickered.

"Actually, I am at her place," I fired back. "We had a really good night, and she's sleeping now." As soon as the words left my lips, I knew I should have kept my mouth shut.

"What?" Jackson roared with laughter. "Let me get this straight. You're at her house after a good night, and she's sleeping? Where are you?"

"On the couch," I muttered.

"Oh, this is classic," he continued to laugh.

"Can I ask, why?" he barked sarcastically.

"I'm not telling you her business," I grumbled. "She had some wine tonight, more than I think she planned on. We talked, and then I helped her to bed."

"And why did you stay?" his voice softened like he might have some genuine concern.

I sighed, "Because I can't seem to leave."

"I get it bro. She's the one that got away, and you don't want it to happen again, but… don't you think she might react badly when she wakes up and sees you're still there?" he chuckled.

"Guess we'll find out tomorrow," I shrugged even though he couldn't see it. "I gotta get some sleep. I'll catch you at work in the morning."

"Later," Jackson hung up.

oooooooo

I don't know what time I finally passed out, but I do know that I was right in the middle of the best dream I've had in a while when I was awoken rather abruptly. "Ahhh!" it was a shrill shriek, and I jumped to a sitting position.

"What?" my head jerked from side to side as I scanned the room for an intruder or something.

"What are you doing?" Kaitlyn stood with one hand held to her chest, and the other was raking her fingers through her hair.

"I was sleeping," I laughed lightly and shifted so my feet were on the floor.

"I see that, but why?" I think it was then that she realized she was only wearing a pair of panties and a cami. "Shit!" she hissed as she turned and scurried down the hall. I then glanced down and noticed I was only in a pair of boxers, that weren't hiding much. My dream had been rather descriptive, and my dick hadn't realized it wasn't real yet. I quickly pulled on my pants and was buckling my belt when she came back into the room.

"Sorry," she covered her eyes, and I laughed.

"You can look. I wear less than this on the beach," I sat back down and then glanced at the clock on the wall. "Shit! Is it really only four o'clock?"

"Yes. I go in at this time every morning to bake," she shuffled into the kitchen and started making coffee. I stood, and followed behind her unable to stay away. It was as if she was a magnet, and I was steel. No matter how much I tried to resist, I needed to be next to her. I sounded like a damn stalker. Jackson was right.

As she poured a cup of coffee, I moved to stand right behind her. I placed one hand on each side of her as I caged her in against the counter.

"Can I have a cup?" I leaned in right next to her ear.

"Yes," she jumped as if she didn't plan on me being so close. She turned in my arms to face me. "Why did you stay, Eli? I need to know?"

"I don't have an answer for that, at least not one that doesn't make me sound like some sort of obsessed man," I skimmed my nose along the column of her neck. Her skin was so soft, and it heated under my touch.

"Mmm," she whimpered.

"Is that an invitation?" my brain went back to my dream. We were in here, and I was fucking her on the counter. I was just about to come when 'real Kaitlyn' woke me up.

"For what?" she whimpered again.

"To stay over more often," I breathed out as I moved closer. I was getting hard again, and I knew she could feel it now. Right as I was about to push things further, a phone rang.

"That's me," she pushed against my chest, and rushed to where hers was charging on the counter. "Hello?" she leaned against the counter. "Shit! Are you sure? I'm on my way." She hung up, and then reached for a travel mug in the cabinet behind her. As she poured her coffee into it, she glanced at me. "Sorry, but you need to leave. There's a problem with one of the ovens at the bakery. I gotta go, and see if I can fix it or get someone in who can. Thanks for everything last night." She rushed out of the kitchen, and down the hall to where I now knew her bedroom was.

"Do you want to some help?" I called after her.

"Thanks for the offer, but I got it," she rounded the corner in a pair of jeans and a Blissful Bites t-shirt. Her hair was pulled up in a knot on top of her head, and she was swiping on lipstick. "Eli?" she motioned to the door.

"I know. I'm leaving. I just feel like I'm leaving you in a bind. I want to help," I grabbed my shirt and tossed it over my shoulder as I shoved my wallet and phone in my pocket.

"You have helped. You helped so much just by listening. Promise," she smiled up at me. "Put that on," she motioned to my t-shirt.

"Why?" I grinned as I flexed my pecs. Her eyes flashed from my face to my chest. "See something you like?"

"It's ok," she laughed as she rose up on her tiptoes and placed a kiss to my cheek. "Thanks again. I'll call tonight."

"I'm counting on it," I winked as I turned and waltzed to my car. I guess I'd have time to shower, and make it in for the fish delivery today since she got me up at four. Too bad we couldn't have picked up where I stopped us last night.

As I climbed in my car, I made mental note to ask Kaitlyn tonight when her next night off was. I wanted to take her on a real date, one where neither of us was cooking and we wouldn't be interrupted. My dick wasn't going to listen to me for too much longer, and I had a feeling that Kaitlyn didn't want him to.

Chapter 11

Kaitlyn

Today has been one of those days that you wish you could just have a 'redo' on. What started out as a nice morning, turned into a nightmare as soon as Ben, my new baker, called with the news about the oven. I'd bought brand new appliances when I opened the bakery, so I had no idea why I would be having trouble after only a few weeks but I was. The bottom element wasn't working, and all of my cookies were burning along with the sweet breads. When I was finally able to get a repairman in, I found out that my other oven wasn't hooked up to the gas line correctly, and I was lucky the place hadn't blown up yet. I'd made a note to call the company that had done my install and give them a piece of my mind.

One of my bakers, who has yet to come clean, stripped out one of the mixers so the beater doesn't spin right. I mean really, can I just have a do over? When I finally was able to leave, I locked up and went straight home. I'm tired, and all I really want to do is talk to Eli. He's working though, so a hot bath is going to have to suffice.

I sent Eli a text when I got home thanking him again, and letting him know that I'll be up if he wants to talk later. I know he's probably going to be tired too, but it would be a nice surprise. I guess he must have thought the same thing, because as I was climbing into bed my phone began ringing.

Hello?" I smiled as I slipped under the covers, and got comfortable.

"Hey?" he sounded tired.

"How was your night?" I adjusted myself and snuggled into my pillow.

"Long. How'd the oven repair go?"

"It was a nightmare. I don't really want to talk about it, ok?" I shifted to my side.

"Sure," there was a lilt in his voice. "Let's talk about something else then. What are you doing right now?"

"I'm in bed," I rolled my eyes. "And you are?"

"Walking into my place. I just got home. Bed huh?" he chuckled. "What are you wearing?"

I laughed. I couldn't help it. This was so childish, but I didn't care. "Clothes, dummy."

"That's not what I meant," he made a tsking sound.

"I know you what you meant, Eli Baker," I groaned in fake annoyance. I couldn't tell you the last time I did this, just talk to a man.

"I'm surprised you have on clothes. I sleep naked," he sighed. I heard what sounded like a door shutting and then keys hitting a counter. "Speaking of, you're coming to bed with me right now. Does it bother you to know that I'm taking my clothes off as we speak?"

"No," I swallowed against the sudden tightness in my throat. "Why would I be bothered?"

"Well," he chucked and I groaned. I'd always thought he had a sexy voice, but his phone voice was dangerous. "This morning you seemed rather distracted with my bare chest. I can't even imagine what the rest of me would do to you. I'm not a boy anymore, Kait. I'm very much a man," his voice sounded almost strained, and I knew he was torturing himself as much as he was me.

"I'm very aware," I sighed as I rubbed my thighs together. This wasn't fair. I'd been fighting the image of Eli sitting on my couch in a pair boxer briefs all night. I was never going to get any sleep at this rate.

"Don't you want to know?" he teased.

"Know what?" I squeaked out.

"What's under the boxers?" his voice sounded breathy, and I wondered if he was pleasuring himself while we talked. I wouldn't blame him if he was. I mean, I was ready to at this rate.

"Nope," I squeaked again.

"You never were a good liar, Kait," he laughed. "Touch yourself. You know you want to."

"Nope," I said it stronger this time.

"Come on. Just like old times," he pleaded. "You'll sleep better. Isn't that what you used to tell me?"

"No," I sounded so small and unsure. The truth was, Eli and I used to do this on a regular basis. In high school, we had much more phone sex than real sex. When you're seventeen it's hard to find privacy. He was right... about all of it. Back in the day, he'd get me so wound up that I'd crash and pass out. Talking like this became a two or three times a week gig in between real dates. "I'm good," I forced the words out as my fingers danced along my panty line. I would not do this. As much as I wanted to, I wanted my first sexual experience with Eli as an adult to be the real thing, not some substitute over the phone.

"Liar," he teased.

"Whatever," I grumbled. "Can't a girl wanna wait until she gets the real deal?" I bit my lip thinking maybe I divulged too much.

"Damn!" his hissed. "Not at all. Listen. When do you have a free night that I can take you out?"

"Next week?" I threw it out there. I didn't really have any free time with the repairs, but I didn't want him to think I was blowing him off either. "I really am busy, but I'm sure we can work something out. I'll come by the bar tomorrow night and hang out for a bit."

"Sure," he yawned.

"I need to get to sleep too. I'll talk to you tomorrow?" I murmured through a yawn of my own.

"Goodnight Kait," that sexy deep sound was back.

"Night," I whispered as I hung up, and turned out the light. It only took me a few minutes to fall asleep.

Over the next two weeks, Eli and I had more of the same conversations. I really was busy, and he was determined to take me out. I thought that our date would never happen until one night when he actually took the entire weekend off for me. We'd have two whole days together, and it scared the shit outta me. What if this didn't work? What if we'd built this up to something that would never be? How would I live up to the Kaitlyn he had in his head, and what did that mean for us?

ooooooooo

Eli

Finally. I'd been waiting for today to get here for the longest time. Kaitlyn and I have been sexting and calling each other every day, and I finally have a real date. I glanced down at my phone again. I'd planned to have today off, but Jackson asked me if I could meet the delivery truck first. Since it was before we opened, I knew I could get away easier. Each load of seafood I helped carry in, brought me closer to seeing her.

Last night had been brutal. I'd thought I'd finally convinced her to video chat with me, but she turned me down. Something about needing to go sleep, and having to bake today. I'd thought she was kidding, but when she rejected my facetime, I knew she was serious. She sent me a text soon after with a sad face emoji, and then this picture that I've been staring at since. It's Kaitlyn, lying on her bed in nothing but a sheet. It's covering just enough that you can't see what you really want too, and it's killing me. I just want to pull the sheet down or push it up an inch, but I can't and every time I start thinking about it, I start to get hard. It's embarrassing, and I've been wondering all day if I should just show up at the bakery and take her in the kitchen.

After signing off on the delivery, I decided to go home and shower. I needed to plan this date, and I wanted to do something nice, but different. I had a few ideas, but I wasn't sure if Kaitlyn would be game for them.

I spent the better part of the day picking up items for my date. A classy bottle of wine, a few French cheeses, some fruit, and then a few surprises that would hopefully not blow up in my face. I'd texted her in the afternoon with the warning that we would be on the beach, and to dress casually, and now I'm just waiting for time to pass as I wear a track on my living room floor.

oooooooo

At five sharp, I headed to Kaitlyn's house. Even though I could have had her drive here, it wouldn't have been a proper date. It took me all of ten minutes to get to her place. She must have been just as anxious as me because when I jogged up her front steps, the door swung open before I could even knock. I almost tripped when I saw her standing there. A dark purple sundress came to just below her knees. It swished around her thighs in the late summer breeze. Her hair was swept back off her face and curled in loose waves down her back.

"Hey," she nibbled her bottle lip as her eyes scanned me from my feet, up to my face.

"Hey yourself," I stuffed my hands in my pockets to keep from touching her. The photo she'd sent me was still fresh in my mind, and I wondered if I'd be able get her to reenact it tonight.

"Let me grab my purse," she reached inside the doorway, and slipped on a pair of leather flipflops, before stepping out to lock up. "All set," she stepped around me and started to go down the stairs. "You coming?" she looked perplexed. It was then that I realized that I was standing there like a statue.

"Un huh," I mumbled as I jumped into action. After helping her in the car, I jogged around and climbing in.

The drive to my house was short, and as I made the final turn toward the beach, I glanced over at her. "I know I promised to take you out, but I'm feeling a little selfish tonight. I don't really want to share you with anyone." I grimaced. "This is my place, but we're going out on the beach." I quickly parked in the driveway, and climbed out as Kaitlyn stared out at the water.

After helping her out of the car, I reached for her hand and entwined our fingers. "It's beautiful here," she mused as I led us over the dunes and out towards the water.

"Thanks," I slipped my shoes off when we reached the sand, and tossed them to the side. I had a small foot wash nearby that I'd had installed when I first bought the house. "You can leave yours too if you like," I pointed to where I'd discarded mine.

"Ok," she smiled as she slipped her shoes off as well.

A little way out, I'd set up a blanket with a picnic basket. Glasses and a wine chiller were sitting in the middle of the blanket to help hold it in place. "Have a seat," I motioned to the soft flannel in front of us. The sun was just starting to sink over the ocean, and it was painting the sky in soft pinks and purples. The beach was practically empty, and the crashing of waves made for a soft cadence in the background.

"I'm impressed," Kaitlyn laughed as she sat down and tucked her legs under herself.

"Why?" I wrinkled my brow as I worked to open the wine and pour two glasses.

"This is really romantic," she shrugged. "You never used to be much of a romantic."

"I was seventeen, Kait. Things change," I knew she was just teasing me, but it stung that she had so little faith in me.

"Sorry. I didn't mean it like that," she sighed as she looked away. We sat there for moment in silence before she turned back in my direction. "I'm sorry. Really. This is" she waved her arms around "scary for me."

"Why?" I handed her a glass of wine.

"Because I want this to work, Eli. I miss you, and I'm scared this is some kind of trick. I'm scared that the last two months have all been a dream, and I'm going wake up from it. I'm gonna open my eyes and realize that I'm still in Paris and I'm miserable."

"It's not a dream, Kait. It's very really," I leaned closer "and I'm scared too. I'm scared that I'm going to wake up one day, and you're going to be gone again. It's happened twice now, and every day I ask myself if I think there will be a third."

"There won't be," she leaned in and kissed me on the cheek. "I can't walk away from you again. I'm in this with both feet, just promise me you are too."

Chapter 12

Eli

"Promise me you are too." The words hung in the air between us. I was in this so deep that I was drowning. I was drowning in my need to be around her. It was all I thought about. I couldn't tell her that though, because that made me sound like some sort of weirdo. "Kait," I took the glass of wine from her hand, and set it down. "I'm definitely in this with both feet." I turned to face her, and cupped her cheek. "I think we're both still suffering from our past selves. We're different now though, right? I know I am."

She pressed her lips together and slowly nodded. "Yes," it came out as a whisper.

"So how about we let the past go? I mean, I don't want to forget it. It's what made us who we are, but I don't want it held against us either."

"I agree," she inched closer. "No more secrets, no more running."

"Hey Kait," I murmured.

"Huh?" she blinked up at me.

"Can I kiss you now," I chuckled. "I've been thinking about it all day, and..." she cut me off as she pressed her lips to mine. It only took a few seconds for the shock to wear off, and then I jumped all in. I mean, nothing was held back here. This was the kiss that the last two weeks had stoked and I had been holding at bay.

I moved my palm to the back of her head, and threaded my fingers through her hair. She sighed, and my tongue took full advantage. She tasted like the wine she'd sipped mixed with peppermint, probably from her lip gloss. It was always a favorite when we younger. Her hands rose up and fisted my shirt, pulling me closer. I couldn't help but oblige as I tilted my head, and swept further into her luscious mouth. My body was waking up, and I groaned as she began to lean back on the blanket pulling me with her.

As she laid back, I used my left hand to hold myself over her. I knew she couldn't support all my weight; my right hand went to cup her shoulder and toy with the strap on her dress. Her left leg bent, and wrapped around my hip as she lifted up and attempted to rub against my thigh.

"Fuck!" I broke the kiss. "Are you trying to kill me?" I smiled down at her as I attempted to catch my breath.

"Why?" a coy smile spread across her lips.

"You little vixen," I teased. "You know exactly what you're doing." I lowered my hips so my throbbing erection would press against her lower belly.

"Mmm," her eyes fluttered closed as she arched her back letting her head fall back.

"How long has it been?" I let my free hand trailed down her body painfully slow. "Kait?" my fingers danced across her thigh until my hand settled between her legs. "You gonna answer me?" I slowly trailed a lone finger over her panties, and watched her tense. I chuckled as I moved my hand back to her shoulder.

Her eyes opened as her lips thinned, "Why'd you stop?"

"Are you pouting?" I snickered as I flicked her lower lip with my thumb. She nodded. "You didn't answer my question."

"A while. Are you happy now? It's been awhile." She rolled her eyes as she pressed against my chest.

"I'm not letting you up yet. You can't start something like this and then just decide to stop. You've done it a couple of times now, and I've let you. I'm not letting you do that anymore," I allowed more of my weight to rest on her as I connected our mouths again. What started out as a feeble protest at best, quickly turned into yearning.

As my tongue plunged in, my hand ghosted back down her side. I gripped the fabric of her dress, and bunched it in my hand. When I felt the elastic of her panties, I released it. With slow, almost painful, movements, my fingers ran across the cotton between her thighs. It was damp and she whimpered.

"I hope you know, this killing me," I murmured against her lips. Her bare foot rubbed against the back of my calf as if she was trying to sooth me. "Anything you're not ready for, you need to tell me," I rubbed my fingers over the cotton again, this time with more pressure.

"Eli," her back arched once more as she squirmed against the ground. All thoughts of stopping flew out of my head as I lifted the elastic at her inner thigh, and let a single finger rub against her skin. It was smooth, something that she didn't do when we were younger. "I'm gonna help you," I mumbled as I tugged at her lip with my teeth. "Relax. Enjoy this," I breathed out as my finger slipped inside her.

"Eli!" she panted as I pressed, twisted, pinched, pulled, anything I could do to make her call for me. It was a rush I hadn't had from her in so long that I forgot what it sounded like. Her body thrashed against me as my dick pulsed against the zipper of my shorts. I needed to be inside her, but I didn't want to be out here on the beach when we did that. It was deserted right now, and almost dark, but I wanted to have her in my bed.

My fingers moved faster as I used the ball of my hand for pressure. Her eyes rolled back, and then I felt it. Every muscle in her lower half clamped down on me like a vise.

Her body went limp and she released a sigh before blinking up at me.

"I'm not really hungry. Can we go inside?" her mouth curled up on one side as I stared down at her in disbelief. "Eli?"

"You don't have to ask me twice," I released her, and straightened her dress as I began grabbing items and shoving them into the picnic basket. "I'm right behind you. Back door is unlocked." I watched as she half ran half skipped up to my back porch. I shoved the bottle of wine in the basket, balled up the blanket, and grabbed our glasses. I looked like a crazed madman as I stalked toward the porch. Both hands were full with our picnic items, my clothes disheveled, and my heart racing. This was the moment I'd been waiting five years for. This is the moment we should have had all those year ago on New Year's Eve. If it hadn't been for the whole marriage thing, I know she would have given in to me. The fact that she didn't, proves what kind of woman she is. She's the staying kind. The kind you marry, not just a good time. Kaitlyn and I had been building up to this since we were kids, and now I needed to slow down and enjoy every moment.

When I reached my house, I shuffled through the back door. I hadn't taken the time to rinse my feet, but they really weren't that bad. I rushed into the kitchen, put the food and wine in the fridge, and left the blanket and basket on the counter. It was then that I noticed Kaitlyn wasn't in eyesight. "Kait?" I called out as I came back into the living room.

"Betcha can't find me?" her sweet voice drifted from down the hallway. In my search, I happen to notice her flipflops by the door.

"Bet I can," I called back as I started down the hall toward my bedroom. When I stepped into the darkened space, I found a trail of clothing items. Part of me searched for panties, and another part of me didn't care. My girl was in my house, and we were finally going to do something I'd fantasized about when we were kids. She was spending the night. All the times we had sex, I always had to take her home. She left before we were old enough to live on our own. We were just high school kids then, but now we were adults, adults that didn't have things like curfews.

"Bet you can't," she giggled again, and I groaned at the sound. When I reached the end of the hallway, I stopped in my bedroom doorway. I propped myself against it by my elbow as I just stared at her. She was parked in the middle of my bed in only a bra and panties, and a beautiful smile. "You found me," she grinned as she threw her arms in the air in victory for me. "But you're way over dressed for this party."

"Oh I am, huh?" I tipped my head to the side, and just smiled. "I think I can fix that," I reached behind my neck, and grabbed the collar of my shirt, pulling it over and off in the process. I tossed it to the side, and then reached for the button on my pants. Kaitlyn's eyes went wide and she licked her lips as I shoved my shorts over my hips.

"That's good," she rose up on her knees. I slipped my thumbs under the elastic of my boxers, and watched her eyes dilate. "That's enough," she swallowed.

"You mean you didn't miss this," I rubbed myself through my boxers. He was throbbing, and confused as to what the hold up here was.

"I did, but I wanna do it," her voice was quiet, almost embarrassed sounding.

"Well by all means," I waved my hands in front of myself, and stepped closer to the bed. "I'm at your mercy right now, Kait. You could tell me to stand on my head, and I would." When my thighs hit the edge of the bed, she rocked up on her knees and crawled closer. When she stopped in front of me, she ran her open palms down my chest. The muscles jumped under her ministrations. Her head tipped to the side before she leaned in, and placed a kiss where her hands had been.

"This is real, right?" she whispered as she kissed me again. "Tell me I'm not in some weird dream, and that we're really doing this."

"It's real Kait. Doesn't this feel real?" I placed my finger under her chin, tipping it up so she faced me. When her eyes met mine, I leaned in, "I've asked myself those things every day since you came back." I pressed my lips to hers and wrapped my arms around her. When my fingers found the clasp of her bra, I released it, letting it fall down her arms. "I convinced myself that you weren't real, that all the times I turned down women for dates it was some other reason, but I was lying to myself. None of them were you, and I didn't want to be let down. They can't hold a candle to you Kait, and I'm fucking scared out of my mind that you're going to change yours, but I can't stay away. You destroying me is worth the risk. Knowing that I have this moment with you, is worth it. Are you hearing me," I leaned down and brushed my lips across hers. "I'm still in love with you."

I watched as the words I'd just poured out to her hit their mark. Her lip quivered as her eyes pooled with tears, "I still love you too." The words were barely audible, but I heard her clear as day. She let the bra fall to the floor as her hands skimmed to my hips. I stayed as still as I could manage as she slowly tugged my boxers down.

When she managed to get them to my knees, I wiggled my legs and tossed them to the side. Standing there completely naked as she stared at me, made me ache for her. Every part of me was wound tight in anticipation, and my cock yearned to touch her. "I can't do this anymore, Kait. I need you so bad right now." I groaned as I attempted to climb onto the bed. She scooted back on her ass until she reached the center. When I climbed over her and started to lean down, she reached up and gripped my neck. No words were exchanged as she forcefully pulled my mouth to her.

I lowered myself beside her as I let her take control of the kiss. Her mouth hungrily devoured mine as her hands moved over my heated skin. It was as if she was trying to memorize me. Her palms slid over my shoulders, chest, abs, and finally down to my cock. As she gripped me, I grunted in satisfaction. It was the first time she'd touched me in over ten years, but she hadn't lost her touch. He remembered her touch, remembered what she felt like, remembered how unsure she was back then.

My hand slid up her thigh stopping at the cotton. "We need to lose these," I mumbled against her lips as I started tugging them down. She shifted back and forth on the bed, helping me free her from the last little bit of clothing between us. I tossed it somewhere behind us, before rolling closer.

The next few minutes went by in a blur. We were all hands, everywhere. I needed to touch her, kiss her, make her feel all the things that I still wanted/ needed from her. I hadn't realized how much she meant to me until five years ago when I found out I couldn't have her. Now that she was here, I wasn't letting her slip away. I planned to make her mine tonight, and if tomorrow led to her realizing we made a mistake, then I'd have to start the process all over again.

"Eli?" she begged as she ground herself against my thigh.

"One second," I rolled toward the nightstand to grab a condom. I hadn't had a woman at my house in over six months. I was lucky I still had some in here. "I'm not ready for parenthood yet," I chuckled as I rolled it on and turned back to her.

"But someday?" her eyes looked sad.

"What? Kids?" I was confused, but then I remember our conversation at her house when she told me that she wanted kids, but Henri didn't. "I'd love to make a baby with you Kait, but I want to make sure we're on the same page." I pressed a kiss to the corner of her mouth.

That was the end of the baby discussion, but I made a mental note to talk to her about again when we weren't right in the middle of making love because that's what this was... making love. I've fucked a lot of women, a lot who meant nothing to me. I've only had a few at the house, but Kait is the only one where real feelings were involved. I truly believe that I've been comparing them all to her, or afraid to have feelings because I've still been in love with her.

I rolled over her, and positioned myself as I leaned down and connected our mouths. "I love you, Kait," I whispered as I pressed forward. She was tight, and the moment took me back to our first time. I'd had to go slow then, mainly because we'd never done it before, but now it was from the amount time since her last encounter. She said it had been awhile, but I had no idea how long that was. "Fuck, you're tight," I hissed as I slid painstakingly slow into her. Her eyes fluttered closed, and when my hips were flush with hers, we both sighed.

"I love you too," she murmured as she cupped my jaw. "Now please make love to me," she smiled softly. With that, I pulled back and pushed forward a little harder causing us both to groan. She felt so good, and the wait was definitely worth it.

I worked us both to the edge stopping each time to pull us back. I chuckled once at the disgruntled look on her face. "Patience," I growled next to her ear. I knew what I was doing. Age and maturity teaches you things, things you didn't know at seventeen. As I sped up, I reached between us and pressed my thumb to her clit. Her back arched, and I knew I'd lost her. She was going over, but not without me. I pumped harder and faster striving for that finish line, and as she called out my name, I jumped with her emptying myself into the condom.

"Fuck! I am so in love with you. There's nobody else for me Kait. You just proven that," I rolled to the side pulling her with me. I couldn't explain it right now, I'd probably scare her, but no other woman that I've been with could hold a candle to what we just did, and no one in future could either.

Chapter 13

Kaitlyn

You know that moment in the morning, when you're right between asleep and awake? That moment where your dreams seem like they could be real? I could live in that moment. When I drifted off to sleep last night, I wasn't sure what the morning would bring and I didn't care. Eli had made me feel loved and cherished. It was something I hadn't had in several years, and I didn't realize how much I missed it. I'd spent so many years settling for what I had, and thinking that I couldn't do any better. Don't get me wrong. When I married Henri, I loved him and I think he loved me. We hadn't been a couple for very long though, and I think we just didn't know we weren't right for one another. I tried too hard, and I think he probably didn't try hard enough. It was both our faults, but he's the one that stepped over the line to end it.

Now, I'm lying here in Eli's bed, listening to his soft snores as the waves crash on the beach outside. It's a warm, comforting feeling, and I'd stay here forever if I could. I can hear him rustling around under the covers, but before I can roll over his arm slips around me and pulls me back to his chest.

"Morning," his voice was gruff with sleep as he nuzzled against my neck.

"Good morning," I yawned. "Your face hurts," I giggled as his morning scruff rubbed against my neck and shoulders.

"You know you love my face," he mumbled as he hugged me tighter. I could feel his erection growing against my ass, and I wiggled it against him.

"Kait," I know he meant it as a warning, but it came out strangled sounding and as more of a plea, so of course I did it again. "You don't know what you're asking for."

I glanced over my shoulder, "Actually I was thinking you could get me all dirty, and then maybe we could take a hot shower, that is unless you're too tired."

"I'm never too tired for this." He rolled away, and I heard the drawer to the nightstand slam, so I was guessing he was getting protection. Before I could roll over, he was back against my back. "Are you sore from last night," he whispered as he gently bit my ear.

"No," I shook my head as he lifted my right leg, and opened me to him. He shifted, and slipped right into me as he draped my thigh over his hip.

"You're going to kill me," he grunted. "I hope you know that, but man what a way to go." No more words were exchanged after that, just grunts and moans with the occasional words of praise. Eli worked us into a sweat before he finally let himself come, and then just like last night, he cradled me against him in a sweet hug. "I love you Kait. Please don't break me again."

It stung hearing those words. I knew I hurt him, but I guess I just didn't know how much until now. He was slowing opening up more and more each day, and I hoped that this time we would make it. This time I'd listen to my heart when it called for him.

oooooooo

"Do you like eggs?" I leaned around the corner to where Eli was sitting with his laptop on the couch. We'd gone from making love in the bed, to making love in the shower, and when he started to go for round three, I requested breakfast. I could stay here all day, which I plan too, but I was starving after skipping dinner last night.

"Kait, have you ever known me to turn down food?" he gave me a 'duh' face from over his screen.

"Good point. Maybe I'll trying something new," I shrugged as his smile dropped and turned into a scowl.

"I thought maybe we were passed that?" he pleaded. I couldn't blame him. When we were first dating, we were still learning our way around a kitchen. I had a really bad need to experiment on different recipes. I'd throw things together to try and invent something new. Eli, being the good boyfriend that he was, was my guinea pig. He'd try whatever I put in front of him, and smile no matter how bad it was.

"Oh come on, don't you trust me?" I called from where I was cracking eggs onto his hot flat top. "I won't give you anything that'll make you sick."

"I've heard that before," he sighed as he went back to what he was working on. He had a point. I gave him fish one time that made him puke all night. I'd felt terrible, but was secretly happy that he'd been the one to try it, and not me.

I grabbed some cheese and the makings for hollandaise sauce before popping some bread in the toaster. I was whistling and not even listening to what he was doing. It wasn't until I felt a hand on my hip and jumped from being startled that I realized he was behind me.

"This actually looks good," he rubbed his stomach when I turned towards him.

"I'm almost finished. Eggs benedict is one of my favorites." I smiled as I plated our eggs. "Here," I handed him his plate. "I had you worried, didn't I?"

"I knew you were kidding," he shrugged as he poured himself a cup of coffee.

"Sure you did," I smacked his arm as I carried my plate over to the couch and made myself comfortable. "Mmm,"

I sighed as I stuffed a bite of egg in my mouth. I was starving.

"You better watch it, or you won't get any breakfast either," he warned.

"Is that a threat?" I teased as I took a bite of toast and did the same thing.

"Nope," he took his own bite. "It's a promise."

"I don't remember you being this horny when we were younger," I sipped my coffee as I stared at him. He was so sexy, and watching him sit there eating in nothing but a pair of flannel pj pants was doing something to me. His hair was tousled from only running a towel over it after our shower, and his jaw was still peppered in scruff. As much as it scratched me, I told him I thought it was sexy this morning, so he left it.

"I was horny," he chuckled. "I was seventeen, and I had a girlfriend that I was banging every chance I had."

"We didn't have sex a lot," I furrowed my brow.

"We were seventeen. We had it as often as we could." He finished his breakfast, and carried his plate to the sink. "I can't help it that I want you, Kait. I finally have unlimited access to your beautiful body. Why wouldn't I want to constantly be with you? I've literally waited years for this." He came to stand in front of me. I smiled up at him, and he leaned over bracing his hands on the back of the couch. "I'd keep you right here if I thought I could," he leaned down and pressed a kiss to the top of my head.

"May you can," I whispered. The idea of staying in this bubble was intriguing, but I also knew that I had a life that I was starting here. I couldn't get so wrapped up in Eli that I forgot my reason for coming back. I was here to start over, and be happy. I had the happy part down, but I needed to be me for a while. As much as I loved what was happening here, I couldn't let that dictate my life.

"Don't take this the wrong way, but I think that might be a little fast," he had a pained expression on his face. "I love having you here, and I love that you want to be here, but we need to get used to us again. You just moved back this summer, and you just got out of a marriage. I want you to want to be here for the right reasons, whatever they are. Do you understand what I'm saying?"

"Yeah, I do," I nodded as I tipped my head back, and pecked his lips. "So what now?" I grinned.

"Now, we run by your place to get some things for you, and then we're spending the day on the beach. I have the weekend off, and you said Ben was baking today." He grabbed my dish and began walking toward the kitchen. "Go put that dress on from last night, and I'll be ready in a few." He began loading dishwasher as I skipped down the hallway toward the bedroom.

ooooooooo

"So you're sure you don't know where they are?" I glanced over at Eli as we drove down the road. We were heading to a more public area of the beach to spend the day swimming and sunning.

"I don't know where they are," he fought the urge to smile. I could see the corner turning up, so I knew he was lying. At least, I thought he was.

"I don't' believe you," I grumbled. "Those were some of my favorites." When I'd gone into his room to get dressed this morning, my panties were missing. I'd tossed the covers around, and looked under the edge of the bed. They were one of my favorites, and matched the dress I wore perfectly. Eli swears that he didn't take them, but I think he did. "Guess I'll have to spend more time at your place to look for them then." I mused.

"I don't mind that," he smiled as he reached over and grabbed my hand.

When we reached the public parking lot, he pulled in and parked. We grabbed our things out of the trunk, and then Eli led the way down onto the sand. It wasn't exceptionally crowded yet, and we found spot not far from the shallow surf.

"I can't believe how nice out it still is. As much as I love the holidays, I'm not ready for the cold," I opened up a sand chair, and sat down.

"The last couple of Fall's have been warm. You've been away for too long. Don't you remember all the times we'd come to the beach after a football game. We'd swim, and then have a fire?" Eli sat the cooler between us, and pulled out a beer.

"I guess you're right," I stared out at the water. There were a few surfers out, and a couple of kids playing in the sand, but that was about it.

"Wanna build a castle?" Eli's brows bounced from behind his sunglasses.

"Aren't we a little old for that?" I laughed.

"Nah. Jackson and Tessa build them all the time. That's kinda their thing. Come on," he stood and rummaged in the bag. "I didn't bring shovels or anything, but if we found a piece of driftwood, we could make due."

"Sure. What the hell," I shrugged as I stood up and helped him look for things we could use.

Once we found a few sticks, and some sea shells, we went to work. I had a hard time concentrating on what we were doing, and Eli caught me a couple of times. It's just, he was so distracting. "You wanna stay over tonight too?" he snickered.

"Maybe," I shrugged as I packed the wet sand. "I'll think about it."

"Seems to me that you already are, I mean with all the staring you're doing. I can feel the hole burning into my back." He stood up, and brushed the sand off his hands. "What'd ya think?"

"I think you need to put your shirt on, that's what I think," I flirted.

"It's hot out here. I don't wanna wear a shirt," he pouted, but all my eyes wanted to look at was his sweat covered chest. "My face is up here," he pointed as he attempted to look at me sternly.

"Un huh," I continued to watch one of the beads make its way down his abs.

"Sounds like you might be a little hot yourself." Before I could stop him, he lifted me, and swung me over his shoulder.

"Eli! Put me down!" I smacked his back which only made him grip me tighter.

"Sure thing sweetheart," he chuckled as he started running toward the waves.

"Don't you dare!" I squealed as the water started splashing up around his legs. He'd slowed down, but was still wading deeper. "I mean it Eli!"

"I thought you wanted me to cool off? That was what you said, right?" his voice held amusement as he dangled me there upside down.

"I never said that. I asked you to put on a shirt," I replied feebly.

"Well I need to cool off for that. It's hot out here," he waded a little deeper, and then paused. "I remember you used to love the water."

"Yeah, when it's hot," I whined. It wasn't cold by any means, but it wasn't hot like the summer either.

"Fine," he sighed as he pulled me back over his shoulder and let me slide down the front of him. When my feet hit the water, I yelped. It was on the cooler side, but not unbearable. He grinned as he wrapped me in a hug. He leaned in, and brushed his lips over mine, making me relax in his arms, and that's when he made his move. "Hey Kait," he whispered causing me to blink up at him. "Hold your breath." Before anything registered, he hugged me tighter, and then flopped to the side plunging us both under water.

"Oh my god!" I screamed as I failed around trying to get my footing. "I can't believe you jus did that!" I scowled at him as I crossed my arms over my chest.

"Yes, you can," he laughed as he shook his head causing water to rain all over us. "Admit it. You like it when I'm playful," he winked and when I didn't give into him, he pushed his bottom lip out into a pout. "Come on Kait," he splashed water at my legs. "Kait?" he came over and stood up in front of me. "You know I'm playing around, right?" he wrapped his arms around me again. "Admit it. You like this." He rubbed his nose against mine, and pressed a soft kiss to my lips. I could feel the ocean water dripping from his hair and lashes.

"Fine," I whispered when he broke the kiss. "I like it when you're playful, but I am so getting you back."

"We'll see," he released me, and then flopped back in the water. We stayed out there until hunger got the best of us, and we needed to eat lunch.

After devouring the sandwiches Eli had packed for us, we spread out the blanket he had, and laid down together to sunbathe. The late night, and water play had completely worn us out. I didn't even realize how much until I fell fast asleep.

Chapter 14

Eli

It's been about two weeks since Kaitlyn and I really started to explore whatever this is. I'm still shocked at how quickly we've fallen into a routine. It's like the last ten years didn't even exist. If I'm not at her place, she's at mine. I'm beginning to think the moving in together thing should happen sooner rather than later. I keep telling myself to slow down, but I can't. I feel like a sixteen-year-old boy that finally got the girl he likes to notice him.

Today's one of the first days that we've spent apart, and it feels really odd. Kaitlyn had to open the bakery this morning, and I'm on the night shift at the bar this week, so we haven't had much time together. Last night Kaitlyn insisted on going home. She claimed that she didn't want to disturb me when she got up to go in, but I think she's worried about not getting any sleep. We don't sleep much when we're together. We've managed to christen pretty much every surface in my house, and we've slowly been working on Kaitlyn's. I'm hoping to get her to come to the bar tonight, and hang out until my shift ends. We both have tomorrow off, and I plan on spending every minute of it with her. I know I sound like a complete sap, but I can't help it. Jackson's told me on more than one occasion that I sound like he used to.

"Do you plan on day dreaming all night, or are you going to help me?" Jackson scowled as he shoved a bus pan in my hands. We're down two bus boys right now. When summer starts winding down, all the students go back to school leaving job openings. We've been interviewing like crazy, but the lower paying jobs are hard to fill.

"I am helping," I grumbled as I weaved between tables, picking up dishes and glasses. "I'm gonna uninvite you tonight if you keep being such a hard ass," I rushed into the kitchen, dumped the dishes on the counter by the dishwasher, and then turned to head back out.

"I'm not missing tonight for anything. I wanna see her in action," he laughed as he smacked my shoulder. "Happy looks good on you."

"Is that supposed to be a compliment? Like I've never been happy before?" I wrinkled my forehead. "I've had lots of girlfriends."

"You've had lots of women go home with you, or to a bathroom stall, or the parking lot," he mused. "You've never had anything that lasted."

"Holy shit, dude. You sound like your wife. Grow a pair." I shook my head as I went back into the kitchen, leaving the bus pan this time. I wiped my hands on the towel that was tucked into my belt before tossing it to the side and heading back to the dining room. Tessa was behind the bar, and Jackson was propped against it laughing at something she said.

"Are you really not going to let us come with you tonight?" she smiled sweetly at me as I approached.

"I guess it's big enough in there that you could come too," I sighed. "Can you keep him under control though?" I laughed as Jackson scowled.

"I think that can be arranged," she grinned at me as Jackson straighten.

"Why is everyone bagging on me tonight?" he pointed at his chest.

"Because it's fun, baby," Tessa leaned over and kissed his cheek. "I need to get back to work. Could you two find somewhere else to measure your dick size or whatever else you're discussing?"

"We both know that mine's bigger," I chuckled and turned to walk away. I glanced back to see Jackson staring at Tessa as she schmoozed a customer. He had this stupid smile on his face, and I realized that when Kaitlyn was around I probably did too. Love did that to you, and while I'm trying to keep myself in check, Kaitlyn is turning me into a love-sick pussy.

Sands of Time
oooooooOo

"That's the last of it," Tessa called as began turning lights off around the bar. "Where's Kaitlyn?"

"Good question," I pulled my phone from my pocket. She was supposed to meet me here an hour ago. I began tapping away to send her a text, as slight unease began to creep in. I wasn't worried yet. I knew something could have happened at the bakery to keep her late. I owned a business. Sometimes things happen that you can't control.

Eli: You ok?

Kaitlyn: Yeah, why?

Eli: You were supposed to meet me here. We're still going to Vibe, right?

Kaitlyn: I thought I was supposed to meet you there. I'm already inside with a booth in the back.

Eli: Stay put. I'm on my way.

I shook my head as I stuffed my phone back in my pocket. "She's already there. Got us a table. Let's roll," I grabbed the keys to lock the front door, and followed Tessa and Jackson outside. "Here. You'll need these for tomorrow," I handed him the keys.

"You wanna ride with us, or are you driving?" he motioned to where his car was parked.

"I'll drive. Thanks though," I jogged over to my car, and climbed in. It was a short drive to Vibe, and I wondered how Kaitlyn got her wires crossed. We'd talked about this several times, and she'd mentioned that she liked hanging out and watching me work. When I got the club, I met Jackson and Tessa by the door. I was in the process of tucking my shirt in as they walked up. This place had a dress code for the men. You couldn't look slobby. Since I'd worked tonight, I'd changed in the office. I couldn't tell if the sweat smell was coming from me, or the club. I'd hoped it was the club, but worst-case scenario I'd be getting sweaty anyway.

"You find Kaitlyn. I'll grab the first round," Jackson waved me off as we paid the cover and entered.

I nodded as Tessa and I began to weave through the crowd. "Bet you never thought you'd get him to kiss you the first time you came here, huh?" I shouted over the loud music as we made our way to the booths in the back. They were half circle style and surrounded the dance floor.

"Nope," she giggled. "Jules had this burning desire to get me laid that night. Guess that's when I discovered mister Bridges had a jealous streak."

"Oh he can definitely be possessive," I laughed as my feet stumbled to a stop, and my mouth hung open. Kaitlyn was sitting on the edge of the booth in what had to be the smallest little black dress on the planet. It was strapless, and pushed her tits up like they were ready to fall out. The bottom barely covered her ass, and the heels she was wearing were definitely staying on tonight when I fucked her.

"Hey!" Tessa waved as she pushed passed me. Kaitlyn stood up, and hugged her hello, but her eyes never left mine.

I stumbled over and attempted to talk, but my tongue felt like a giant lead weight in my mouth. "You like it?" she blinked innocently up at me.

"Um," I cleared my throat. Fuck yeah, I liked it, but so did every other guy in the place. "Do you want to see me get into a fight tonight?" I leaned closer to her ear so I wouldn't have to shout.

"Payback sucks doesn't it?" she kissed my cheek before sitting back down, and acting like she wasn't trying to get me hard at the moment. It was then that I remembered what she'd said on the beach. She was going to get me back, and I wouldn't know when. I wasn't thinking it was going to be something like this, but I'll be the first to admit that she's as much of player as I am when it comes to one uping each other.

oooooooo

Kaitlyn

This was fun, plain and simple. When I'd sifted through my closet, I'd forgotten that I even owned this dress. Henri bought it for me when we attended a dinner together with some of his friends. When I'd moved back, I'd hidden it in the back of my closet. Seeing things that he'd purchased for me still hurt. This was perfect for tonight, though. When I'd gotten dressed, I'd stood in front of the mirror and that's when I made the decision to come here instead of the bar. If I'd met Eli at work, we never would have left. He would have seen the dress, and kept us in. That would have spoiled all the fun, so I changed the plans.

"Glad you like the dress," I leaned next to him as I sipped my martini.

"You're so mean," he mumbled as he sipped his beer.

He wasn't doing too bad himself tonight. I knew he'd worked, but he'd changed from his regular dress shirt and kakis. Tonight, he was wearing dark jeans and a black fitted t-shirt. The sleeves were rolled tight on his arms, and he'd added a gray beanie that I've never seen before.

"Is this a new look?" I smiled as I placed my palm strategically on his upper thigh.

"It's a 'I was sweating at work, and my hair's a mess' look," he chuckled and then stiffened when my hand drifted toward his cock. "What are you doing Kait?"

"Remember when you dunked me in the ocean?" I skimmed my lips up his neck and paused beside his ear "I'm just getting started."

"Let's dance!" Tessa laughed as she stood from table across from us.

I pushed against Eli to get him to let me out, "Sure. I'm game." I smiled sweetly at him, "you don't mind, do you?"

"Go ahead," his voice was tight, and I could tell he was still trying to recover from what I'd been doing under the table.

Tessa and I weaved our way through the crowd out onto the dance floor. I glanced back a few times to see Jackson and Eli deep in conversation. On more than one occasion, Eli would glance up thinking I didn't notice, and stare at me. If everything went according to plan tonight, I'd have him so wound up, that we'd have a night we wouldn't forget.

"He's crazy about you, I hope you know that," Tessa shouted next to my ear as we started to move to the music. It was a low sultry beat.

I lifted my hands above my head, and closed my eyes as my body swayed. It was hot, and my hair was sticking to the back of my neck. "Are you trying to kill me?" his voice sounded almost threatening as his body pressed against my back.

"Hey!" Tessa squealed as Jackson appeared behind her. He whispered something in her ear, and she nodded and followed him off the dance floor.

"I could ask you the same thing," I sighed as I pressed back against his chest. I could feel his heartbeat thundering against my back, and his cock hardening against my ass. I never listened to the warnings about playing with fire, so of course I wrapped my arms around his neck, and ground my ass against him. He hissed, and his hands flew to my hips.

"You won't win this battle, sweetheart," he nipped at my ear. "I control when you come tonight," he growled as one hand left my hip and slipped around to press against my belly. His pushed his hips forward, grinding into me, and my patience snapped.

"Eli," I tried to turn around, but he held me in place.

"Sucks doesn't it," he snickered as his hands began to glide over me. "Losing control. I find it funny that you thought you had it in the first place." His chin dipped as his lips moved along my shoulder and neck. I couldn't help by groan in frustration. He smelled so good. He had to have put on cologne before he left, and his shirt smelled like whatever soap he used. I was addicted to the stuff, and had been planning to buy some just keep at my place so I could sniff it whenever I wanted to.

"I need," I sighed as I attempted to turn again.

"Getting a little frustrated, are we?" he chuckled as he turned me to face him. He made sure he kept us close enough to keep his obvious erection hidden. He placed his knee between my legs as he pulled me closer. God, I was so worked up that I was ready to jump him right there. It didn't matter that we were in the middle of a club surrounded by people. I wanted him. I wanted him more than I wanted air at the moment. Between the three martinis I'd consumed, the sexy music that was like foreplay, and then the way he looked and smelled... I was a goner the moment he walked in. Now, I was dealing with the fact that I'd tried to get the upper hand here. If I knew Eli, he wasn't going to forget that, and I'd be paying for all night.

"Can we get out of here?" I slipped my hand between us, and cupped him through his jeans. "I have a plan for this."

"You do, huh?" he breathed against my cheek.

"Mmm hmm," I bit my lip as I glanced up at him. His eyes darkened, and he released me twining our fingers together. "And for the record," I tugged to get him to lean down "I like this version of you. It gets me wet," I moaned against his ear. That was all it took. Eli made a beeline for the door, practically dragging me behind him. I didn't care though, I'd been waiting for this since we first got back together. I love the sweet side don't get me wrong, but I want the grown-up version of Eli Baker. I want the man that takes charge, and makes women beg for him. I want the Eli that I kept hearing about when I first came back.

Chapter 15

Kaitlyn

When we reached the parking lot, Eli stormed in the direction of his car. I tugged against the grip he had on my hand, "I'm parked over there."

"We'll get your car tomorrow. Get in," he opened the passenger door, and motioned to the seat.

"Bossy much?" I blinked up at him and attempted to look innocent. He muttered something under his breath, but I couldn't make it out. I climbed in, making sure to stick my ass in the air, and heard him groan. After he slammed the door shut, he rushed around to the driver's side, and climbed in. He sat there for a moment, breathing heavy and white knuckled, before he cranked the engine. "You ok?" I turned in my seat, and placed my palm on his thigh.

"I'm fine," he ground out as he began backing out of the parking space.

As we began our drive to his house, I slowly moved closer. "I think I have a solution for your problem," I mused. Without giving him a chance to push me away, I reached over and lowered his zipper.

"Kait?" he warned.

"Watch the road," I reached in and freed him, and heard him hiss. "Hands on the wheel, or I stop," I commanded before leaning forward, and taking him into my mouth.

"Shit!" he hissed again as the car swerved slightly. "You're going to get us in an accident."

I licked up one side and down the other before swirling my tongue around the tip. "You have a really pretty cock. You know that?" I mused as I blew across the tip.

"Fuck, Kait. You're killing me here," he growled as I ran my tongue up the underside. I leaned down, taking in as much of him as I could before hollowing my cheeks, and sucking hard. His hips started to lift off the seat, and I pressed down on his thighs. When he settled back down, I tugged the zipper lower, and parted the fabric. One hand continued to pump his cock, as the other cupped his balls. His breathing became ragged as I pumped and licked, sucked and massaged, but I wasn't stopping. I was going to get him back for what he did on the dance floor. I was in control right now, and I think he may have been too afraid to turn me down at this point.

"Kait," he warned. I glanced up and noticed that we were at his house, but the car was still running and if I wasn't already worked up enough, Nine Inch Nails "I Wanna Fuck You Like an Animal" came on the radio. I rocked up onto my knees, hollowed my cheeks once again, and doubled my efforts, "Fuck. Kait. I'm gonna. I'm gonna come." I sucked again. "Kait, are you…okay…in your…fuck!" He roared as he climaxed, and I sucked every last drop from him. He went lax in the seat, and I hummed in satisfaction. I ran my tongue around the tip, cleaning him up before I carefully tucked him back in his jeans. I moved back to my seat before glancing over, and seeing a satisfied smirk on his lips. "Do I even wanna know where you learned to do that?" he sighed.

"Probably not," I shrugged as pressed my lips together to keep from laughing.

I watched as Eli opened his door, and waltzed around to my side of the car. He had a stupid smile the entire time, and I felt slightly proud that I was the one to put it there. He opened the door, helped me out, and then leaned down next to my ear. "I hope you don't think that all of that," he motioned to the front seat "gets you out of all of this," he motioned to the house.

"Mmm nnn," I shook my head. "I'm counting on the fact that it doesn't." I winked at him as I stepped in front of him swaying my hips all the way to the door.

"Vixen," he muttered under his breath as he followed me, stopping only to unlock the door.

Sands of Time
oooooooo

Once inside, Eli dragged me, by the hand, back to his room. He slapped at the switch by the door causing the overhead lights to illuminate the room. "That's better," he gave a quick nod. "Come here," he pulled me in front of himself, and then positioned us in front of the full-length mirror on his wall. "I've been teased and tortured by this all night. You see all of this?" he ran the back of hand over my jaw letting his knuckles just gaze my skin. "This is fucking perfection, and I honestly don't know how I got so lucky." One arm was wrapped around my waist, pinning my back to his chest. I could feel the heat from him radiating through my dress. He was calmer now, probably due to the fact that I'd pleasured him, but his actions and words were promising anything but a mellow night.

"I don't like being teased Kait," his fingers grazed my neck making their way down to where my breasts were heaving from my heavy breathing. "I need to see this." He reached up with both hands, gripped the top of my dress, and tugged it down causing them to fall out. "Beautiful," he sighed as he cupped them. "These are mine," he pinched the nipples sending a zing straight to my center. I was so wet at this point that it was down right embarrassing. "This dress is only to be worn when I'm around. Do you understand?" he plucked at my nipples causing me to rub my thighs together. I needed friction. I needed something.

"Yes," I whimpered. "Please Eli?" I squirmed in his arms.

"I told you," he chuckled. "I decide when you come tonight." His palms left my breasts, skimmed down my sides, over my hips, and began bunching the bottom of the dress. It climbed higher and higher until he slipped it up over my ass. He stepped back, and appraised me offering a satisfied grunt. "Very nice," he smacked my ass. "This can stay," he plucked the string of my thong before slipping his hand around the front of me, and pressing against the lace. "You seem a little worked up, Kait," he mused. "Regret teasing me yet?" he chuckled again. "As much as I love this, it's getting in the way." He lowered the zipper of the dress, and carefully removed it, tossing it over a chair in the corner.

Here I was a whimpering mess. Dressed only in my heels and a thong, wound tighter than any spring on the planet, and at the mercy of this man. This sexy, surprisingly dominate, beautiful man. "Can you turn the light off?" I whispered.

"Nope," he laughed. "I wanna see your face when I finally let you come." He looped his finger under the edge of the thong and used it to tug me toward the bed. He leaned into me pausing at my ear, "You tell me to stop if I go too far. Promise me that." His voice was sincere. This was the man I loved, the one who loved me, but he was trying to give me another side of him. He wanted me know that he wasn't going to push me. I had control, even though he was the one asserting it.

"I promise," I nibbled my lip.

"Don't do that," he reached up and used his thumb to free it before leaning in, and pressing his lips to mine. The kiss was slow at first, but when I parted my lips, he dove right in pushing us to an almost frantic pace. His arms banded around me, his head tipping to the side, as his tongue plundered the dark corners of my mouth. It was erotic and surprising all at the same time. What else was he hiding, and why the hell did we wait so long. Eli was the perfect mix of passion and dominance.

We stumbled backward until my thighs hit the edge of the mattress, and he gave me a light shove. I fell back, bouncing when I landed on the plush bed. Eli's mouth curved up on the side, as he reached behind his neck, and tugged his shirt over his head. It was tossed somewhere off to the side, and then he stepped out of his shoes. I licked my lips as his hands went to his belt. "You wanna see this again, don't you?" I nodded a little too eagerly for him, and I watched his eyes darken. His jeans soon hit the floor along with his boxers, and before I knew it, he was climbing over me. "I don't like to be teased Kait," he warned as he fisted his cock, stroking himself a few times. His head fell forward, and a groan slipped out between his lips. I was throbbing at this point, and just about willing to do anything to get him inside me.

"Eli?" I reached out and attempted to touch him.

His eyes snapped open, and his head slowly shook from side to side. "I told you. You come when I let you." He leaned down on all fours and crawled over me. "I'm gonna fuck you so hard that you're going to feel me for days, Kait. You're going to be icing that pussy after tonight," he made his way down my body, and leaned in to bite the inside of my thigh causing me to yelp. He pressed a kiss to it, to sooth the sting before he moved closer, and slipped his hand under the thong. "This is mine," he whispered as he pushed the lace to the side. "Only mine." His head dipped down, his hands pressing my thighs apart, as his lips grazed over me.

"Eli!" I squealed. He laughed as his thumb slowly parted me, and he ran his tongue over my clit. "Oh shit!" my back arched when he sucked causing me to just about lose it. A finger slipped in, teeth nipped, and those lips... Oh my god those lips worked some sort of magic.

"Na uh uh," he pulled back just as I got to the edge. "I'm not ready for that yet." I looked down at him thinking he was kidding, but he wasn't. He was backing away from me, just staring at what he'd done. I was soaked, and he wasn't doing anything about it. "Sucks doesn't it?" he wiped at his mouth. I grunted in frustration as he slowly climbed back over me. "I told you. You come when I decide." He grabbed his cock and rubbed it over the center of the thong pushing the lace against me and giving me a tiny bit of friction. As soon as I started to climb again, he stopped. I punched the bed beside me, as he laughed. "Ever heard of orgasm delay?" he mused. "It's going to make this so much better."

He pulled the thong to the side, and rubbed himself over me, "Are we good Kait? Can I do this, or do you want me to get a condom?" He paused and the old Eli, the one that I knew so well emerged. "I promise I'm clean. I haven't been with anyone bare in years."

My eyes went wide, and I fell just a little harder for the man he'd become. "We're good," I cupped his cheek. "Promise. I trust you."

As soon as the words left my lips he transformed right before my eyes. "Eyes up here," he commanded as he pushed the thong to the side, and entered me. "Mother fucker," he hissed as he slowly pushed forward. "I love how tight you are, but this feels so much tighter. I feel all of you Kait, and you feel so fucking good right now." His head dipped, capturing a nipple in his mouth as he slowly pulled back, and then sank back in. As he began to pick up speed, I started to climb once again. The tingling began in my feet, and made its way up my body. His hands were everywhere, his lips sliding from my breasts to my neck, up to my ear. "You feel that Kait? You feel how fucking hard I am?" he moved faster, and right when I started to crest, he froze in place.

"What?" I blinked as I watched his lips curve into a knowing smirk.

"Not yet," he brushed my hair back and pecked my lips. "You're not ready."

"Oh, I think I am," I whined as my body slowly fell back down the hill.

"No, you're not," he began to move again, but this time faster. Sweat broke out over his entire body. His thighs flexed with his movements. His hips were pounding into me with such force, we were sliding up the bed. "Look at me Kait," he commanded as he moved faster and faster, stroking deep inside me. My body woke back up, climbing once again for the peak, only this time he let me reach it.

White spots appeared in my vision as I crested over the top, convulsing as I went. I was so lost in my own moment, that I failed to notice Eli's. When I looked up at him, his head was drooping between his shoulders, his body shaking with the aftershocks of what had to be his own powerful orgasm.

"I fucking love you so much," his kissed me. It was slow, passionate, and completely contradictory to the sex we'd just had. "Thank you for trusting me."

"I love you too," I kissed him back as I brushed his hair off his sweaty forehead. "And you were right… delayed orgasm is so much better than I ever could have imagined."

Chapter 16

Eli

I think today was the first day that it started to feel like fall was on the way. It was cool outside with a crisp breeze in the air. Business was beginning to slow down, and as much as I liked it to stay busy it was nice having a slow day. This was the time of year that most of our employees went back to school, or left the area for the winter. We stayed open year-round, but we only had a handful of workers that stayed on with us. Most of our waitstaff only came here for the summer. I had three kitchen staff that stuck around, and Tessa kept four bartenders on.

When I showed up this morning to help Jackson open, he was grumbling about business being slow. I was usually the one that did this, but now that I was spending time with Kaitlyn, I liked a slow day. Slow days meant we could close early if we wanted, and I wasn't exhausted when I left. Don't get me wrong, we need business to stay open, but we've been open enough years now that we have savings to fall back on if we have an off month.

"So I was thinking," Jackson glanced up at me from behind his computer. We were both working in the office today before the dinner shift. I needed to switch over from our summer menu, to our standard one, and Jackson was balancing out the expense reports with our smaller staff.

"That could be dangerous," I laughed as Jackson scowled. "Sorry, go on."

"You know," he shook his head at me "You've turned into quite the smartass now that you're getting some."

"What can I say? She makes me happy," I shrugged as I rocked back in my chair and crossed my foot up on my knee.

"Happy looks good on you, Bro. I'm glad you worked it out. Anyway, I was thinking that maybe we could do some seasonal desserts this year. You know… something pumpkin for the fall, and then maybe something peppermint for the winter?"

"Ok," I tapped my fingers on my chin. "I could come up with something new, I guess." I've always liked experimenting in the kitchen, I just never really have time. Now that the kitchen is slowing down, I could stay late a few nights and see what I come up with. "What kind of prices are you looking at for these new creations?"

"Something similar to what we have for the summer. I don't want to send our costs through the roof with some exotic fruit or spice that we have to special order, but I want to add something that we can promote and help bring in business."

"Things aren't bad, are they?" I rocked forward and steepled my hands on my desk.

"No, not at all. I'd like to keep it that way though," he clicked his mouse a few times. "I've got to submit the new table cards to the printer by the end of the week if we want something before Labor Day. You think you can have a ballpark idea of what you're going to do by the weekend?"

"I guess," I grimaced. I'd wanted to spend the weekend with Kaitlyn, but experimenting in the kitchen held a close second to her. "That's only five days."

"I just need a name for what you've picked, and a picture. You can tweak it afterwards. Keep the holidays that people come here for in mind as you're building these. Thanksgiving, Christmas, New Year's, and St. Patty's Day. I figure we can go back to the standard items after that. The summer crowd starts showing up around Memorial Day."

"Sure. Ok. Let me think about this tonight, and I'll start throwing some things together tomorrow." I jotted down a few items that I'd need from the store because we don't keep them in regular stock here, and then went to check on my staff. They were supposed to be working on the chowder for the evening, but the last time I left the newbie in charge, he burnt it and tried to cover it up. I pride myself in my kitchen. Whatever comes out of it, is a direct reflection on me. Sam, my sous chef, is great, but he's off today. When he's not here, I have to be the one to check over everyone else's shoulders.

oooooooo

Kaitlyn

Today was a great day. We've been open for eight weeks, and business is still booming. Crescent Moon Beach was the perfect place for a bakery like Blissful Bites. I'd found a good rhythm, now I was able to go home in the evenings instead of running myself ragged baking into the wee hours of the morning. My staff was reliable, and Ben was the best hire I'd made. He shared my passion for baking, and his skills were top notch. Things really couldn't get any better right now.

After closing up today, I'd gone home to shower and found myself restless. I usually played around in the kitchen when this happened. Some of my best recipes came from being bored, but as I pulled the brownies I'd made out from the oven, I realized that it wasn't helping. I missed Eli. It'd been less than twelve hours since I'd left his house, and I was craving the attention he gave me. After waking up in his arms this morning, I'd gone to work, stiff and sore I might add, and now I just wanted to climb back in his bed. We'd decided this morning that we both had stuff to do today though, and we'd see each other tomorrow. That idea sucked, and I wondered what he'd done to convince me that it was a good idea.

I quickly sliced the brownies, piled them on a paper plate, and covered them in cling wrap. I glanced down at my leggings and oversized sweatshirt, and shrugged. I was clean and comfortable, and I had chocolate. Good enough in my book. I laughed at myself as I slipped on pair of shoes, and grabbed my keys. I hadn't planned on going to the bar tonight, but what the hell. I could use some soup and a drink as an excuse, and I knew Eli would never turn me away.

ooooooooo

When I got to Anchor Bay, I grabbed my brownies and made my way to the bar. It wasn't as busy as it usually is, but it was also a Monday. Mondays are always slow in restaurants. If you ever want to go somewhere nice and not have to wait, go on a Monday. Anyway, I took a seat and ordered a glass of chardonnay. Tessa smiled as she handed me a menu, and then disappeared into the kitchen. I'm assuming she went to tell Eli that I was here.

"Hey," he smiled when he came walking out. "What are you doing here?" he leaned in and kissed my cheek.

"I came for the soup. I really like it," I grinned as I sipped my wine.

"It's chowder tonight, and that hurts," he pouted as he pressed his fist to his chest.

"I brought you chocolate," I smiled sweetly as I lifted the paper plate towards his face. "They're fresh."

"Yum," he sighed as he sat them to the side. "I might use those later."

"Later?" I turned on my stool to face him.

He stepped between my legs and hugged me, "I have to come up with some new desserts. Might do something with brownies. Women like chocolate, right?"

"What does that have to do with anything?" I furrowed my brow.

"It's usually women that order dessert. Even when the man eats it, it's usually because his date ordered it. If I want a successful menu, I need to pick things women like," he stepped back. "I might be a little scarce this week until I figure this out."

"I could help," I sat up a little straighter. "I mean, I do own a bakery. We make desserts and stuff," I pressed my lips together as I grinned at him.

"You really wanna hang out here cooking after you've been at the bakery all day?" he tipped his head to the side.

"Sure," I shrugged. "I get to spend time with you, and I love experimenting. You should know that by now."

"Ok," he chuckled. "I'll see you here at ten tomorrow night."

"Ten?" I grimaced.

"See? I knew you'd be tired. The kitchen closes at ten. We have to do this after the kitchen closes," he laughed.

"Ok. Ten it is," I gave a quick nod. "Now go get my chowder," I shooed him toward the kitchen door, and giggled when he saluted me. I wasn't too keen on being here late, but if it meant playing around in the kitchen, I was game.

oooooooo

Today seemed to drag by. Business was steady, but the lines at the door seemed to slow down. Customers were figuring out the best times to come to avoid the crowds, and I'd come up with a system on what to bake and when. We'd just gotten in the ingredients needed for my pumpkin spice muffins, so I knew business would pick back up to the crazy level once the word got out.

It was rather blustery today for early fall, but I was loving it. This was my favorite time of year besides Christmas. The leaves started to change, football season was back, and nights snuggled under a blanket with Eli were in the future. Bon fires on the beach were one of my favorite things, and now I actually had a man that would indulge me.

When six rolled around, I helped Brenna and Chloe close up, and then headed home. I wanted to take a shower and maybe a short nap before heading to Anchor Bay. Who knew how long Eli would want to work tonight. He was working the dinner shift the rest of the week, so unlike me, he could sleep in.

Since it was on the cooler side, I dressed myself in layers. Leggings, an oversized tee, and a hoodie. It would get warm in the kitchen with the oven going, but I hated wearing coats. I always waited until I could no longer stand the cold before dragging my coat out of the closet.

When I pulled up to Anchor Bay, the parking lot only had a few cars in it. The lights were dim inside, and the 'kitchen closed' sign was hanging on the door. I heaved the heavy door open to find a lone bartender serving a handful of what must be regulars at the bar. She smiled at me as I waved and made my way to the kitchen. When I peeked around the corner, it was empty, and I frowned. Did I get my wires crossed? Were we meeting at a different time? I took a few more steps down the hall until I came to the office. Jackson was sitting behind his desk, so I knocked to make my presence known.

"Hey. Where's Eli?" I stepped further through the door.

"He got a phone call. I think he stepped out back to have some privacy," Jackson mumbled as he stared at the screen of his computer.

"Ok. Thanks," I waved as I turned and meandered toward the end of hallway. There was a heavy door propped open at the end, and I could hear Eli's voice coming from outside. He sounded angry, but I couldn't make out what he was saying. "Eli?" I stuck my head out, and was shocked find to a cold expression on his face.

"I can't talk about this right now," he growled angrily into the phone. "Bye." He clicked off the call, and then transformed right in front of me.

"Everything ok?" I crinkled my brow and twisted my lips as he moved closer.

"It's fine. Just a delivery that's screwed up," he shook his head as he helped me open the door and stepped inside. "Give me a second, and I'll meet you in the kitchen."

"Ok," I headed back to the kitchen as he went to the office. I heard him say something to Jackson before coming back out and following me.

"I've got a list of some ideas I'd like to try here," he tossed a note pad on the stainless-steel counter. "Your brownies made me think we could make a whiskey drizzle and use that with ice cream for St. Patty's Day. I want to do something with pumpkin for the fall, and then maybe peppermint for Christmas. All I really need is an idea for Thanksgiving."

"What about something with cranberries?" I popped my hip out to the side before leaning against the counter. "I have a couple of sweetbreads that I make with cranberries. We could use that in a sundae of sorts, or even make a cheesecake. Women love cheesecake," I grinned.

"Great," he sighed.

"What? I thought you wanted desserts that women would like. The other day…" I trailed off.

"I know what I said, and you're right I'm just having a rough night," he turned in the direction of the walk-in cooler, and yanked it open.

"Need some help?" I stepped away from the counter but he held up his hand halting me. In a matter of seconds, he reemerged with an arm load of butter and eggs.

"You can start that sweetbread recipe while I get what we need in dry storage," he tossed the items on the counter, and stormed off around the corner. I knew that offering to help didn't seem like the right thing at the moment. He didn't want it for some reason, and I really didn't know my way around this kitchen.

"Are you sure you're ok?" I grabbed a bowl from under the counter and started cracking eggs on the side. "You seem like you don't want me here."

"I'm fine," he dropped the things he was carrying onto the counter, and then rounded it in a few quick strides. "I'm glad you're here," he growled as he banded his arms around my waist. "I like cooking with you." He slammed his mouth into mine, and completely caught me off guard with a heated kiss. His tongue forced its way in, as he slanted his head and devoured my lips.

"That didn't feel like fine, Eli," I whispered as he broke the kiss. "That felt like something else. An apology maybe?"

"I just missed you today, and…and nothing," he waved his arms in the air as he rushed back to where he'd left the bag of sugar he'd brought out.

"Fine," I mumbled. Something was off, but I wasn't going to push him. I had things I was still dealing with, and I'm sure he had the same. One day in the near future I was going to make him talk to me though. We had to be able to communicate if we wanted this to work, and I so wanted this to work. I wanted it to work so badly that whatever he was hiding was eating me alive at the moment. It was scaring me to the point that I was afraid it was the first chip in the very foundation we were trying to build.

Chapter 17

Eli

Last night went better than I planned. With Kaitlyn's help, I managed to construct an entirely new dessert menu. We'd stayed, trying new recipes, until around midnight. I felt bad that she was going to have to go into work in the morning after helping me all night, but we had fun nonetheless. I haven't felt this good in a long time. Between the revolving door of one-night stands, and the few that have lasted more than that, I've never really felt happy. I thought I was at one point, but then Kaitlyn came back and proved me wrong. The others were just place holders as I waited for her. Not knowing if we'd ever have a second chance kept me on edge, and closed off. Now that we're here, together, I feel like a kid again.

Just last night we had a flour fight in the kitchen. Jackson came rushing around the corner when he heard the commotion, and got a face full of flour. Kaitlyn had been the one the throw it, so he forgave her. I think if it had been me, I would be more than just tired. Jackson and I have only gone to blows once, and it was enough. He has a mean right hook. When Kait left, she was covered in flour, I tried to convince her to come home with me and shower, but she insisted that she needed sleep and she wouldn't get it at my house.

oooooooooo

"Here," I tossed the list of names for my desserts on Jackson's desk. It was almost time for the dinner rush, and I was exhausted. "I sent you pictures that I took last night before we destroyed the kitchen."

"Thanks," he set the list to the side. "You look like you stayed up all night."

"I kinda did," I sighed as I hung my jacket across my desk chair, and grabbed my chef's coat.

"What? Why?" he stopped what he was working on and looked at me.

"She won't stop calling me. I think I need to change my number," I muttered as I buttoned the coat.

"Have you tried talking to her? Maybe you just need to…" I held up my hand to cut him off.

"I'm not talking to her. There's nothing to talk about. Please drop it," I turned and left before he could say anything else. I knew Jackson meant well, but I wasn't entertaining this idea any more. I had a life, and she wasn't part of it.

"Hey boss," Sam waved as I rounded the corner. "We're all set for the night."

"Great," I smiled as I took my place at the expo line. Now that business had slowed down, I could work the pass through and let Sam run the kitchen more. It made my nights less hectic, and Denny, the new guy, seemed to listen to Sam better. I don't know why, but I didn't care either. If everything ran smoothly, I was a happy camper.

Tonight's shift seemed to drag by. Kaitlyn wasn't going to be coming in, and that had been something I'd gotten accustomed to. It was like clockwork. The kitchen would slow down, and she'd come sit at the bar and have a glass of wine. Most nights it was slow enough that I could come out and say hi. Last night though, she'd mentioned having dinner with her parents. I couldn't blame her. In the six months she'd been back, she'd only seen them a handful of times.

It was funny the way she did it, like she was afraid I'd get mad or something. She kinda tossed it over her shoulder on her way out the door last night. I'd laughed at her, and then gave her a hug and sent her on her way. I've always gotten along with her parents, and if she'd asked me, I would have gone with her. I don't think she's told them that we're back together though.

I've been daydreaming for the past hour, just thinking about what she might be doing right now. It's killing me.

I've never craved time with a woman like I do Kaitlyn. "Hey Eli," Tessa's head popped around the corner. "You have a visitor at the bar," she nibbled her lip like she was afraid of how I'd react.

I laughed. Kaitlyn couldn't give it up. She must have finished dinner early, and decided to come here anyway. "I'll be out in a minute, Tessa," I smiled as I wiped my hands on the towel tucked into my waistband. I chuckled to myself as I made my way around the corner, and froze in my tracks. The visitor at the bar was most certainly not Kaitlyn. Why was she here? Did all the unanswered calls last night not send a clear message? Did my chilly response when I did answer the phone not help?

I stood there in the shadows of the hallway just watching her. She was sipping on what looked like water, and talking to the guy on the stool beside her. Her hair was pulled back, and a pink sweater accentuated her tits. She looked a lot like Kaitlyn from a distance. It's what drew me to her in the first place, but now that the 'real' Kaitlyn is back I can see that there is no comparison.

Tessa's head happened to pop up from where she was concentrating on mixing a drink. Our eyes connected, and I slowly shook my head 'no'. She tipped her head to the side in confusion before going back to what she was doing. I, on the other hand, turned on my heel and went right back to the kitchen. I had no desire to talk to *her,* and I doubt I ever will.

oooooooooo

"You ok?" Jackson stepped into the kitchen the next morning. I'd come in to meet the delivery guy since sleep had been evading me.

"I'm fine," I snapped as I pried open a crate of oysters.

"If you say so," Jackson shook his head. "You know I could have done this today, right?"

"I know that. I was trying to be nice," I grumbled as I began tossing the oysters into the sink and running water over them. They were the special today, and this batch seemed to be abnormally sandy.

"Tessa said she showed up last night. You better deal with that before she comes on a night Kaitlyn's here. What did she even want?" Jackson began helping me sort the oysters.

"I have no fucking idea. I haven't seen her in months," I rolled my eyes. "I told her the last time she called that I wasn't interested anymore. That we were over. I thought she got the message. She didn't call after that until the other night," I shook my head as I let my chin drop to my chest.

"I'm telling you Bro. You need to talk to her, and you need to make sure she gets the message before Kaitlyn gets it instead," he squeezed my shoulder before leaving me standing there in the kitchen.

I had no desire to talk to Tracy, but he was right. What if Kaitlyn had been at the bar. What if she'd seen her? Would she notice that she looked like her?

oooooooooo

Kaitlyn

It was official. I was crazy about him. Eli invaded every moment of my day, from the moment I climbed out of bed to the moment I fell asleep, sometimes he even invaded my dreams. I spent last night at my parent's house. I'd casually brought up the idea that Eli and I were seeing each other. My parents tried to acted surprised, but my dad couldn't keep up the act. He'd finally told me that he knew as soon as I moved back that it wouldn't take us long. My mom, on the other hand, was concerned that I was moving on so quickly after Henri and I split. The truth is, it is fast, but Henri and I were over long before I left. I think we both just didn't know it at the time.

After having breakfast with my mom, I came home for a quick shower, and now I'm heading to the bakery. My dream keeps growing, and today I was getting ready to add another thing to my list of what I've accomplished. I got a call yesterday for a wedding cake. I've been wanting to design one on my own for years. I've always helped, but this was my chance to prove I could do this.

After filling my travel mug with coffee, I decided to walk to work. My house was only a few blocks away, and the nice weather wasn't going to be around for too much longer. The leaves were already changing, and soon it would be too cold to walk.

When I got to Blissful Bites, Brenna mentioned that Denise, my bride, would be there at noon, and she booked a baby shower cake appointment for three. I thanked her as I went into the back to start making a few tasting cakes. I had three in mind that I wanted Denise to try, but then I wanted to add one more. Chocolate and vanilla were pretty standard, but then I usually made a carrot cake, and a red velvet. With the wedding being a fall wedding, I wanted to mix up one of my cranberry spice cakes too. It always gave a little color for when you cut into it. Denise wanted something large enough to accommodate her seven-hundred-person guest list, and I was trying to keep cost in mind. I wasn't the most expensive wedding cake designer in the area, but I wasn't cheap either. My cakes were one hundred percent edible including the sugar flowers, and that took time. When it drew closer to wedding day, I'd be busy for several days straight constructing and decorating this.

After baking my tasting cakes, and frosting them complete with fillings, I carried them out to the table I'd been using for appointments. It was off to the side, but allowed me to have some privacy without being in the back. I arranged the cakes, and placed forks on the table, one for the bride and one for the groom if he decided to come. I placed my sketch pad, and calculator across from the cake, and grabbed some bottled waters. The cakes taste so much better if you can cleanse your mouth in between flavors.

At noon sharp, Denise came in smiling with another woman. They looked very similar so I assumed she might be a sister, or cousin. "Hey," I waved. "So good to see you again, Denise. Have a seat."

"Thanks Kaitlyn. I brought my sister, Annie, to help me decide on a flavor," she rolled her eyes, as her sister bounced over to the table. She had to be at least a few years younger than Denise's twenty-two.

"I've got four choices here for you, but if there's something else that you want me to include, just say the word and we can do it. I can pretty much make any flavor, it's just that these are dense enough that they'll stack better." I sat down across from her. "This is a dark chocolate truffle cake with raspberry mouse filling," I cut a slice for each of them to try.

"Oh my god," Annie sighed as she slowly chewed the cake. "This is soooo good," she elbowed Denise. "You totally need to pick this one."

"It's just the first one," Denise laughed as I cut a slice of the next choice.

"This is a vanilla sponge cake with lemon curd filling," I pushed the plates in front of the them and reached over to take what was left of the chocolate.

"Do you have too?" Annie pouted as she reached for her plate with the chocolate.

"Nope," I smiled. "The chocolate is my favorite too."

"This is good. How am I ever going to choose," Denise whined slightly as I cut the next one.

"This is a carrot cake with cream cheese filling," I slid that over as I cut the last cake. "And this is a cranberry spice cake with a whipped brown sugar filling."

"How do you stay so tiny with all of this around?" Annie looked perplexed.

"When you're around it every day, you don't want to eat it," I laughed as I began picking up plates. "Well, what do you think?"

"I think I'm in trouble. I like them all, but I like this one the best, and I think it goes with the theme of the wedding the best," she pointed to the cranberry spice cake, and I clapped in excitement.

"I'm so glad you like it. This is a new flavor here, and I almost didn't put it out as a choice." I pushed the remainder of the tasting cake toward her, "Would you like to take the rest of this home?"

"Yes," Annie grabbed the cake as her eyes went wide.

"Don't mind her. She's home on fall break, and has only been eating cereal for the last week of classes," Denise giggled.

I grabbed my sketch pad, and moved my chair closer to them. "What were you thinking for a design?"

"My colors are a gold and burgundy. I was thinking maybe something that has that ribboned look? You know, like the band of ribbon around each tier with a bow?" Her brow furrowed as I began drawing. As fast as she could get the words out, I was sketching a barebones version of the finished product. "Maybe some crystals here and there to make it sparkle? It's an evening wedding, so it needs to be fancy."

"Like this?" I showed her my drawing. "Gold here, and burgundy here," I labeled the sketch. "See that display cake? That's a sugar bow. Do you like that?"

"Perfect," she clapped as she bounced in her seat. Her eyes glistened with happy tears as I jotted down a few notes.

"With the guest list size you have, I'm thinking at least six tiers, maybe seven. I need to pull my pans out and see. If you want something taller, we could even put a few dummy tiers in to get the height."

"That sounds perfect," she smiled as she pulled out her check book.

"I need a $150 deposit for today, and then the balance will be due the week before the wedding," I smiled as I filled in the spots that were still blank on her contract, and then signed before handing it to her to sign.

"Thank you so much," she scrawled her name across the bottom, and then handed it over.

"No, thank you. I look forward to making this beautiful cake for your wedding. It's a privilege," I held out my hand to shake hers, and then grabbed my things to clean up and get back to work. Denise and Annie bought a few cookies, and then waved happily as they left.

When I stepped back in the kitchen, and out of sight, I did a little happy dance. This was what I had been waiting for. This moment. I've dreamed of being the next big thing, and this wedding was just the first tiny step in what I hoped would be a very successful future.

Chapter 18

Kaitlyn

"So how was your day today?" Eli and I were currently sitting on my couch pretending to watch tv. He had my feet in his lap, and was rubbing them.

"Busy, but busy is good," I groaned as he dug his fingers into my arch. "That feels good. You have to come over every night now."

"That could be arranged," he shifted and reached for the other foot.

"I'm gonna hold you to it then," I laughed lightly, but it turned into another groan. "I had two more consultations for cakes, and then I had the pie orders start coming in for Thanksgiving. The next two months are going to be insane."

"You know I can help some, right?" his fingers started dancing up my calves.

"I appreciate it, but you have a life too. I have employees to help me," I giggled when he hit a particularly ticklish spot. Just as I was getting ready to say something else, Eli's cell started bouncing around on the table in front of us. His head jerked to the side, and even though he tried to hid it, he looked upset. "What's wrong?" I attempted to pull my foot away.

"Nothing," he reached for the phone, and clicked ignore all the while tossing is back on the table. "Where were we?" he smiled as he tugged on my legs, bringing us closer together. I was practically sitting on his lap now, and I rested my head on his shoulder.

"If you need to go, just go. I run a business too. I get it," I murmured as I nuzzled into his neck.

"It's not work, it's a wrong number that keeps calling me back," he sighed as his palm slid up my thigh and rested against my hip. "Just forget about it, k?" he hugged me tighter, and we settled back into the couch. Within a few minutes the buzzing started up again. "Holy fuck!" he growled as he reached for the phone, clicked ignore for the second time, and then started furiously texting.

"What are you doing?" I sat up and tried to see the screen.

"I'm texting the fucker who won't leave me alone, and telling him I'm not the person he's looking for," Eli hit send, then tossed the phone on the table. "I'd fucking turn the thing off if I wasn't worried that someone might need me at work. Jackson's done that before, and I've gotten screwed because of it. I would never do that to him," he grumbled as he relaxed back into the cushions.

"I'm sorry," I reached up and ran my fingers through his hair.

"It's not your fault," he mumbled as he leaned into my touch. "Are you even watching this?" he motioned to the tv.

"Not really. I had it on more for light than anything else," I laughed lightly. It was dark in the house, and I didn't have a street light nearby, so when the sun went down, it was dark.

"I kinda like the dark," he murmured as he deftly pulled me the rest of the way into his lap, and simultaneously turned off the tv. As the remote hit the table, Eli's lips attacked mine, and the constantly vibrating phone was ignored.

oooooooooo

Eli

When morning came, I had to sneak out of Kaitlyn's house. She had the day off, but I was on mornings again. I left her a note by the coffee pot telling her I loved her and would see her tonight, and then stuffed my keys and phone in my pocket and slipped out the door. I didn't like doing this, but I wanted to let her sleep. She's been so busy lately, that she deserves it.

Once I got in my car, I dared to look at my phone. "Fuck!" I roared as I punched the steering wheel. I had twenty-two missed calls. What the fuck was Tracy doing, and why the hell wasn't she getting the message that I didn't want to talk to her. Showing up at work was one thing, but now she's calling nonstop and fucking texting.

Unknown caller: I need to talk to you

Unknown caller: I really need to talk to you

Unknown caller: Please talk to me

Unknown caller: This is important Eli

Unknown caller: I'm going to keep doing this until you talk to me

Unknown caller: Do I need to talk to your girlfriend?

That one got me. I did not need Tracy calling Kaitlyn. I hadn't done anything wrong. Tracy was an on again off again woman who I liked to fuck. She looked a lot like Kaitlyn, so it helped ease the pain after she left again, but I broke things off as soon as Kaitlyn came back. I knew that Tracy would never fill the void completely, and I needed to be with the real thing. Tracy seemed accepting at first. I didn't hear anything from her. It was only about a month into the relationship that she started in with this.

First, it was showing up accidently at the same places we were. I was able to leave without letting on to Kaitlyn. Then the calls started. I ignored her at first, but then made the mistake of answering at the bar that night. I thought for sure that Kaitlyn was going to hear us when she came outside to find me. Now, the texting and calling, won't stop. My phone blows up all the time with messages from her. I don't know what she's trying to accomplish. I don't want to be with her. She was a fuck buddy. She served her purpose, and now I don't need her anymore. It sounds harsh, I know, but she came into the arrangement knowing this already. We talked about it before anything happened. That seems to be the problem with some women, you're up front with them yet they think they can change you, and make you want more. The truth is, I do want more just not with her.

Against my better judgement, I call her back. It's early, and she's probably still sleeping, but I don't care. After last night, I don't give a fuck about niceties.

"Hello?" her voice is groggy and heavy with sleep.

"You need to stop fucking calling me," I barked into the phone. "I don't want to talk to you. I don't want to see you, and you need to leave my girlfriend out of it!"

"You won't talk to me. What else was I supposed to do, Eli?" she sighed. "I need to tell you something."

"Like what?" I rolled my eyes. This was her routine. She found a way every time I called to get me to see her in person. It was this way when we were fucking, and now it seems it's this way when we're not.

"It's important, Eli," she began to whine. At one time I found this cute, but now it was just getting on my nerves.

"I have to work this morning," I growled.

"What about tonight. You could come over, and we could talk. I'll cook you dinner," she had a bit of a desperate edge to her voice.

"No. I'm not coming over. We aren't together anymore, and I'm with somebody," I huffed. "You need to let that go."

"We were good once," she whined again.

"That ship sailed months ago, Tracy," I paused for a moment. Jackson was right when he said I needed to talk to her. If she keeps this up, she's going to ruin Kaitlyn and I. "I'll meet you at three at Endless Joe's," I sighed. "This is your chance Tracy. Don't blow it." I clicked off the line, and turned the key to start my car. In the back of my mind I knew meeting her was a mistake, but I'd convinced myself that this was the only way to get rid of her.

ooooooooo

Work was unusually busy during lunch today. I ended up jumping on the line to help Sam keep up with the orders. When the crowd finally started to die down enough for me to go into the office it was already close to time for me to leave. I needed to leave by two-thirty at the latest if I wanted to meet Tracy on time.

Jackson was in his usual spot in the office. Lately he'd been spending most of the day in there. Dinner shift he would work the dining room, but otherwise he was at his desk. "Must be nice," I grumbled as I removed my chef's coat and hat.

"You're the one that wanted to run the kitchen," he chuckled. "I knew that job wasn't for me. I'm a numbers guy." When I didn't respond, he closed his laptop and rocked back in his chair. "You ok?"

"I'm fine," I sighed. "I didn't get a lot of sleep last night, and before you start in on that it wasn't because of Kaitlyn."

"I wasn't going to say anything," he held his hands up in surrender. "What's going on. You've been off for days."

I paused in the doorway, took a few steps further into the office, and closed the door. "She's still calling me," I sounded defeated, I knew it.

"Tracy?" Jackson's eyes bugged out.

"Yeah." I blew out a deep breath as I stepped around my chair, and flopped down into it. I glanced at the clock, and noticed that I really didn't have time for this, but I didn't care anymore for some reason. Maybe it was the fact that I was still mad. I don't know.

"What the fuck man? What the hell does she want?" he leaned closer as he stared at me.

"I don't know. She called me twenty-two times last night. I was with Kaitlyn. Do you know how hard it was to pretend like it was nothing?" I ran my fingers through my hair.

"Did you tell Kaitlyn about it?" he rocked forward and shoved his chair back.

"No," I ran my palms down my face.

"Bro. You need to tell her. This is going to blow up in your face."

"I know I do, I'm just not ready for this to end yet," I sighed.

"Why do you think it's going to end. You didn't do anything wrong," Jackson flung his arms out. "Not telling her is what's going to end it."

"I'm meeting Tracy today for coffee. I'm going hear her out and then I'm telling her to get the fuck out of my life," I shook my head in disgust. I was so angry, more at myself for letting her into my life than anything.

"Well I hope it works out for you, but I still think you need to talk to Kaitlyn," Jackson slid closer to his desk, and went back to work. "If you want to grab a beer later, just let me know."

"Thanks man," I waved as I stood, and left.

ooooooooo

Endless Joe's was a coffee shop a few blocks down the street from the bar. I used to take dates there when I had no intention of going out for a meal. It was a common meeting place for each party to decide if they wanted to continue the casual hookup. It's where I met Tracy.

Suggesting we meet there today was my way of taking that final jab at her. After what she'd been doing to me, I didn't feel guilty at all.

When I pulled up, I parked in the back. Not that Kaitlyn ever came this way, but if she did, I didn't want her to see my car here. Tracy was sitting in the back, sipping a water when I entered the coffee shop. I waved off the barista as I made my way to the back table. "Hey," Tracy smiled at me, but I didn't reciprocate.

"What do you want?" I yanked the chair out, and sat down.

"I thought we could sit and talk for a little bit," she pressed her lips together, and played with the straw in her water glass.

"Well you thought wrong. I don't want to be here, Tracy. I'm here because you're forcing me. Do you get that?" I kept my voice low. I didn't want an audience.

"So that's how it is," she nodded.

"Yes. That's how it is. Now if this was all a ruse? Then I'm done," I started to get up, but her hand flew out and grabbed my arm.

"It's not," she looked panicked. I slowly lowered myself back into the chair. "Remember that time we went to the wharf? I got really sick the next day, and you thought it was weird that you didn't get food poisoning because we shared our food?"

"Yeah, sure," I really didn't remember, but that wasn't uncommon. We only ate together a handful of times, but our relationship turned more sexual. At that point it was more about fucking than dating.

"It wasn't food poisoning," she released my arm, and placed her hands in her lap.

"Ok," I still didn't get it. "You've been blowing up my phone to clarify that," my brow wrinkled.

"I'm pregnant, Eli," her lip trembled as she rubbed her belly.

"It's not mine," I shook my head. "No way. I wore a condom every time," my head spun as I spewed any words that would come to mind. This wasn't fucking happening right now.

"It has to be. There hasn't been anyone else. Protection fails. It's on the packages as a warning," tears started to fall from her eyes, and where I should have felt sympathy, I felt anger.

"You did this on purpose. You're trying to trap me. It's not mine," I shook my head.

"It is," she slowly stood, and I could see the small bump behind the cotton top she was wearing. "This baby is ours, and I expect you to help me. I'm gonna tell her if you don't," her eyes narrowed.

"You leave Kaitlyn out of this!" I warned.

"I have an appointment next week. There's going to be an ultra sound. I expect you to be there," she slapped a small piece of paper down on the table in front of me. "If you're not, then I'll call your girlfriend. She runs Blissful Bites, right?"

"Tracy," I warned again.

"You may not want this baby, but he's coming and I didn't make it on my own," she grabbed her purse, and started walking towards the door. "See you Tuesday, Eli," she called over her shoulder causing the knot in my chest to grow tighter. Fuck!!! What had I done?

Chapter 19

Eli

"So she just blurted it out like that? I'm pregnant!" Jackson and I were sitting at the bar at Vibe. I needed to go somewhere to clear my head, and I knew it would be loud enough in there that no one would eavesdrop on us.

"Un huh," I sighed as I reached for the shot glass of amber liquid in front of me. I lifted it to my lips, tossed it back, and motioned for another one. The bourbon burned as it made its way down my throat to settle in my stomach. I'd been at this for over an hour, and I was pretty closed to being trashed.

"I think you might want to slow down," Jackson warned.

"Easy for you to say. You're not staring at impending fatherhood," I tossed back another shot. It was then that the words I'd just said sank in. "Oh shit. I'm sorry Bro," I turned to face him. "I'm drunk, and I'm mad. I didn't mean..." I trailed off as Jackson shook his head.

"It's ok. I know you didn't mean it like that. The truth is, being a dad is one of the best things in the world. I'd give anything to be a dad again. As soon as Tessa's ready, we're going to start trying. I get why you're scared, but being dad doesn't have to be the end of everything." He sipped his beer. "This happened before Kaitlyn. It wasn't planned, but you didn't do it to hurt her. I can't believe she isn't being more supportive."

"She doesn't know yet," I took another shot. "She's waiting on me to come over tonight so we can talk more about moving in together. I've fucked this up so bad, and she doesn't even know it."

"You need to tell her. She might surprise you," Jackson clapped me on the shoulder.

"I'm not telling her anything until I know if it's mine. I don't trust Tracy as far as I can throw her." My head spun slightly from the alcohol, but I motioned for another shot. When the bartender looked our way, Jackson called her off.

"You've had enough, Eli," he tossed a few bills on the bar. "I'll take you home."

"So are you my Dad now?" I rolled my eyes as my anger at Tracy was now being directed at him. "Stop telling me what to do. You have no fucking idea what it's been like for me. We had a plan, and she left, and I fucked it all up," I shouted causing a few people around us to notice.

"Let's go," he wrapped his arm around me and started ushering us to the door. "I'm driving," he grabbed my keys out of my hand as he stopped by the passenger door to my car. He jogged around to the driver's side, and climbed in. "I know you're hurting right now. I know you're mad, and confused. I know that I'm here, and that's why you're mad at me, but you need to talk to Kaitlyn. You're still mad at her for leaving you all those years ago. You may think that things are fine now, but they're not. You just proved that. If you don't work things out now, you'll always resent her in some way."

"Don't you think that I'd talk to her, if I thought I could? Things are good with us now. If I bring all this up, it's going to make them not good," I leaned back in my seat as the world spun around me. "I need to puke," I flung open my door before Jackson stopped completely and hurled on the side of the road.

"You need to sleep this off," Jackson sighed. "You're rambling, and not making any sense. Promise me you aren't going to call her tonight."

"Un huh, Supposed to go to her house, 'member?" I muttered. I could see Jackson shaking his head out of the corner of my eye. The truth was, I had no intention of doing anything over the phone.

When we pulled up to my house, Tessa was waiting with her car. Jackson must have texted her before we left so, she'd come get him. "I'll see you tomorrow. Go sleep it off. Tell Kaitlyn you're not feeling well," he put the car in park, removed the keys, and took them with him.

"I need my keys to get to work tomorrow," I rolled my eyes as I stumbled out of my car.

"Right. You promise me you aren't going to do something stupid, and I'll leave them," he held them out in his hand in my direction.

"I never do," I tried to look innocent, but I know he probably saw right through me. "I'm going to bed," I stuffed them in my pocket. "Thanks for the drinks."

"Later," Jackson waved as he climbed into Tessa's waiting car, and watched me shuffle to my front porch. It took me a few tries of tripping up the steps, but I made it.

oooooooo

Against my better judgement, I dialed Kaitlyn's number. "Hello?" she sounded half asleep. "Eli? Are you ok? I thought you were coming over?"

"I need to see you," I slurred into the phone. "Please come over here." I stabbed my keys at the front door, attempting to get them in the lock.

"Are you drunk?" I could hear sheets rustling, and my dick started to harden at the thought of Kaitlyn in bed.

"Nooooo," I snickered into the phone. "I'm locked out of my damn house," I grumbled as I tried again to get my keys in the lock.

"It's two in the morning. What are you doing outside?" something jingled, I'm thinking maybe her keys.

"I was out with Jackson, and I can't get inside. I need you to help me get inside with these keys. They don't want to work, and these are the wrong keys…I think, maybe. Come help me please," I knew I wasn't making sense, but my bourbon-soaked brain thought I was.

"I'm coming," she yawned, and I could hear her shoes clicking on the concrete outside.

"Damn right you are," I snickered again.

"Eli?" she huffed. "Is this a bootie call? Are you really even locked out?"

"Yes, to all of the above," I chuckled. "Now hurry up before I have to take care of myself on the porch."

When Kaitlyn clicked off the line, I turned and pretty much fell down trying to sit on the steps. Since I couldn't get my keys to work, I figured I didn't have much of a choice, and thinking about Kaitlyn coming over in her pjs made my semi go to full mast. I didn't need my neighbors seeing that.

It didn't take long for the headlights to appear. She pulled up, cut the engine, and climbed out. As she walked toward me, I noticed she was wearing a pair of sweatpants, and tee. "What is this?" I motioned to her.

Her brow furrowed, "You asked me to come over and open your door."

"No, I mean this?" I motioned up and down in front of her. "You don't sleep in this. I woke you up. You're supposed to come as you were, not changed."

"Eli," she slammed her hands on her hips. "I sleep naked."

"I know," I wiggled my brows as her face flushed.

"Give me your damn keys," she held her hand out as she rolled her eyes.

"Fine. Suck the fun out. Fun sucker," I grumbled as I slapped the keys in her palm. "They don't work," I sighed as she opened the screen door, and slipped the key in the bolt lock on the wooden door. I heard a click, and then Kaitlyn pushed the door open and stepped back. "How'd you do that?"

She turned to me all straight faced, and then burst into laughter. "Are you for real right now? I unlocked it. Your keys work fine," she grabbed the front of my shirt and pulled me through the door.

"Oh, good," I threw an arm over her shoulders and leaned in. "I need to properly thank you." I nibbled at her ear, but before I could kiss her, she pushed me away.

"What's going on?" she crossed her arms over her chest, and the moon light that was coming from the front window made her glow like some sort of angel, an angel that could save me.

"Nothing," I murmured all playfulness gone. "I had a bad day. God, I need you Kait." I moved closer, wrapping my arms around her. "Please stay," I pressed my lips to hers "please don't push me away," I whispered against her lips. "Say you'll stay." I hugged her tighter, begging her to stay with me all the while moving us farther into the house. "Please?"

She paused for minute, but then relaxed in my embrace and I knew I'd won, "I'll stay."

oooooooooo

Kaitlyn

I don't know what happened at the bar tonight, but there was a desperation to his movements. As he pushed us through the house, and towards his bedroom, he tugged at his clothes as if they were burning his skin. We left a trail all the way to the bed, and then he attacked me, literally. Desperate hands skimmed over my sides as eager lips peppered my neck and face. His voice quivered as he entered me, and with each thrust he begged me to never leave. Apprehension filled me as a sense of foreboding seem to fill the room, but I pushed it aside. He was drunk, and I was letting his rollercoaster of emotions swamp me.

"I love you so much. Please don't go, Kait," his grip tightened on me as he half kissed, half nipped at my lips.

Sands of Time

Each thrust of his hips brought on more pleading, and I just surrendered as I attempted to be what he needed. I didn't know where it was coming from, but the scars I had from ten years ago were slowly reopening as I witnessed what leaving truly did to him. He'd never been vulnerable in front me, and witnessing it was slowly killing me.

"I won't. I promise. I love you too, so much," I cupped his face, ran my fingers through his hair, scored my nails down his back. I was trying to mark him like he was marking me. I needed him to believe me. I wasn't going anywhere. I was his, and he was mine. "Do you hear me, Eli? I love you!" I whispered the words just as desperately back to him as his body shuddered emptying itself into mine.

He sagged against me, his breathing ragged, before wrapping his arms around me and rolling us to our sides. "I won't make it without you," he murmured as he slowly drifted off to sleep leaving me puzzled as to what brought all this on. I'd never seen him like this.

As I attempted to fall asleep, my head filled with scenarios that would cause this to happen. Was I fooling myself to think that we were ok? Was it all a ruse? What could have possibly happened at work to make him want to drink like this? The 'what ifs' swirled inside me until sunlight peered through the curtains. Eli was softly snoring, his arms still wrapped tight around me. Dampness coated the sheets and my thighs as evidence of the night before. My eyes slowly drifted shut as my brain finally reached the point of turning off. If something was really wrong, he'd tell me, right?

Chapter 20

Eli

My head pounded as I chopped the onions for the chowder on today's menu. I shouldn't have drunk so much last night, but I needed it. I needed to escape for just a little while, even if it was only for a night. The morning had been quiet, thank god, and no one bothered me. Jackson wasn't coming on until the afternoon, so I didn't need to worry about the lecture I was sure to get from him. Sam was in the kitchen sorting through the day's shipment, and I was on chowder duty. I didn't mind. It was mindless work that I could do with my eyes closed. I had a call in already from one of my line cooks, so it looked as if I was working a double today.

"All set in here," Sam leaned around the corner. "Lobster looks good this time. You wanna run the crab leg special again, Boss?"

"Yes, thanks Sam," I nodded and then made a mental note to not nod anymore today. My brain was pulsing against my skull, and I thought I might puke.

"I'll get that ready, and then start prepping the clams," he waved before walking off and leaving me there.

"God damn," I muttered as I squeezed my head. This was not going to be a good day if the morning was like this.

ooooooooo

Lunch was surprisingly busy today, and I'd almost forgotten about how I felt until the cause of my problems came walking in. Standing in the middle of the restaurant, her eyes met mine, and she offered a tight smile.

I sighed, as I motioned toward a table in the back. The far section of the dining room wasn't open during the day, so I knew we could get some privacy if we sat back there. She followed me without saying a word, and took a seat.

I stood. I didn't want her to think that this was okay by any means.

"What are you doing here, Tracy?" I stuffed my hands in the pockets of my dress pants.

"You didn't show up today," she shifted in the chair, and glanced up at me, an angry resolve set across her features.

"I never said I would," I rolled my eyes in annoyance.

"I guess I'm going to have to take matters into my own hands," she pinched her lips together.

"Why?" I shrugged. "I don't want to be with you. If this kid is mine, which I don't think it is, it's not going to make me be with you." I flung my arms out to the side. "You say it's mine, fine. How? The timeline doesn't match up."

"What do you know about babies?" she balked. "It's yours Eli, and I expect you to step up," she crossed her arms over her chest and pouted, a look I used to like. Now, it just annoys me.

"I don't want to come to your appointments. If this kid is mine, I'll be there for it, I guess," the sick feeling from earlier was slowly coming back the longer I stood there and talked to her.

"What do you mean, you guess?" she looked shocked.

"I mean I don't want a kid," I shrugged. "I still don't think it's mine. We used protection every time. How could it be mine? Do you know the likelihood that it could happen?" my voice was getting louder and louder by the minute, and I soon began to worry that someone might hear us.

"It happens," she looked disgusted. "I haven't been with anyone else," her lip curled in disgust that I was even making the insinuation.

"Right," I nodded as I took a deep breath.

"What's that's supposed to mean?" she shrieked.

"It's means," I took a deep breath before I laid into her. I knew that I probably needed to walk away, but I couldn't. She was trying to ruin my life, and I couldn't stop the words coming out of my mouth even if I wanted to. I was angry, and I was at the point where I was going to say whatever I could to hurt her. "The first time you and I fucked was ten minutes after we met. I took you into the bathroom, and fucked you against the wall. I'm sorry if I don't truly trust you."

"You're an asshole," I felt the sting against my cheek before I realized that she'd slapped me.

I cupped my cheek to ward off the sting, and then straightened to deliver the final blow. "And yet you still fucked me," I shrugged as my head tipped to the side. She stared for a few seconds just standing there before turning on her heel, and storming off toward the door. "Don't let the door hit you on the way out," I called to her retreating back. I laughed when her hand flew up in the air with her middle finger pointing at the ceiling.

oooooooo

Kaitlyn

This morning has been a blur. After oversleeping and having to run to the bakery without getting a shower, it's been one appointment after another. Word got out about my cakes, and I've had two more brides book appointments. I had a bridal shower appointment this morning, and a walk in that wanted to order a custom birthday cake. I've literally been so busy that I haven't eaten anything yet, and its nearly four in the afternoon. I was just getting ready to head into the back to grab my lunch when another customer walked in the door. Brenna had left for the day, and Chloe was in the bathroom, so this was on me.

"Hi. Welcome to Blissful Bites. Can I help you with anything?" I called out as I finished putting my note pad and custom schedule book away.

"Maybe," the woman shrugged as she perused the cooler in front of me. I had a few cupcakes and pies in it, but mainly cookies. "I'm looking for ideas for a baby shower," she murmured.

"Oh, congratulations," I smiled as I now noticed her visible baby bump. "How far along are you?"

"Six months," she rubbed her stomach as she moved closer. Her face didn't radiate the usual happiness of an expectant mother, and something inside me told me to watch out, but I couldn't figure out why.

"What kind of flavors do you like?" I grabbed the notebook I'd just put away.

"The father's favorite flavor is lemon, so I was thinking of using that. You know men, they don't get much say in this type of stuff," she kind of laughed, but the smile didn't reach her eyes. "I was really hoping he would come with me today, but he had to work."

"I hear that," I nodded as I watched her drag her hand along the counter. She kept glancing around, and the same foreboding feeling from the night before began to fill me. "Did you want to take a few cookies with you, and maybe schedule an appointment to come back when your husband can come with you?" I grabbed a small box off the back counter.

"No thanks," she sighed. "I doubt I'll ever get him to come with me. He's not really happy about the baby. It's funny," she laughed lightly "he enjoyed making it, just not actually having it."

"I'm sorry," I tried to sound supportive. "Maybe he'll come around."

"Maybe," she shrugged. "We're not married though. He's kinda a big deal around here. You may have heard of him. He owns the bar two blocks over, Anchor Bay?"

Blood whooshed in my ears causing me to feel light headed. I heard her, but I couldn't believe her. Surely Jackson wouldn't cheat on Tessa, and then the words I was dreading finally fell from her lips.

"...Eli Baker..." her lips continued to move, but all I could do was stare. "You know him, don't you?" her smile turned slightly sinister as she placed a piece of paper on the counter, and shoved it in my direction. "Can you give him that for me? I forgot to when I stopped by earlier." Without another word, she turned and left leaving me standing there in stunned silence.

Completely numb, I reached over and grabbed the paper she'd left. In the corner were the words 'patient Tracy Clawson', and in the middle was a grainy black and white image of a baby. It had it's hand in the air as if it was waving, and then a small arrow pointing down with a typed message that said 'I'm a boy'.

I stumbled backwards until my back hit the counter behind me, and then as the tears began to fall my legs gave out and I slid down until my butt hit the floor. How could he hide this from me, and what's worse...? I mentioned having a baby some day and he seemed petrified of the idea. How could he have a baby with her?

ooooooooo

"Are you ok?" Chloe rushed over when she saw me on the floor. I nodded, but didn't move. "What are you doing down here?" she squatted down.

"I felt a little light headed," I mumbled as I slowly pushed myself to a standing position. "Can you close up for me tonight. I think I should go home," I turned without waiting for an answer, grabbed my keys, and left through the back door.

I don't know how long it took me to get home. I was going through the motions without actually doing anything. My house felt foreign, and when I sat down on my couch, I just stared at the blank tv. The seconds turned into minutes, the minutes to hours as the sun sank behind the trees. In the darkness of the living room, I heard a boom of thunder just before lightning zipped across the sky. It was a perfect comparison of what I was now feeling. My heart cracked a little more with each rumble of the sky, and as the rain began to fall, pelting my windows, my tears joined in tandem. I don't know why he hid this from me, or what he thought he'd accomplish by lying, but Eli was not the man I thought he was. I don't know how long I sat there, but as evening became night, I curled into a ball, and tried to keep my fragile heart from shattering more.

oooooooo

Eli

When the kitchen finally started to slow down for the day, I couldn't wait to go see Kaitlyn. I needed to hold her, and ease the turmoil that was slowly raging out of control within me. I was so conflicted over the whole Tracy situation, that I wasn't sure how to react. Did I believe her, or was this just a way for her to try and get me back? I'd thought I'd been clear when I ended things, and if this baby was mine, why wouldn't she have told me then?

I stopped by the office to let Jackson know I was leaving, and then sprinted to my car to attempt to stay dry. The storm was now raging. Waves crashed against the pilons as trees bent under the gusting winds. This was hurricane season, but according to the weather channel this was just a bad storm. I thought about calling first, but decided stop by the bakery instead. Kaitlyn usually worked late during the week, and should still be there.

I pulled up along the curb at the front, but the lights were off. It was odd, but not uncommon. I sighed at the realization that I was about to get soaked. I flung open my door, and ran around to the back. The kitchen was back there, and if she was baking, she would be too. As I jogged around the building, I was met with the same situation, no lights. I leaned up against the brick, hoping that the slight overhang would offer some protection as I fished my phone out of my pocket. I quickly dialed her number, but was sent directly to voicemail. Either she was on another call, or her phone was off. Neither seemed plausible, but whatever. When I heard the beep, I smiled. "Hey baby. I'm standing out here in the rain. I was hoping to surprise you, but I guess the surprise is on me. Call me when you get this, and I'll come over." I hung up, and made a mad dash back to my car.

Just as I slipped behind the wheel, I felt the vibrations of a text coming in. I laughed as I pulled it out, but the sound quickly died when I read the text.

Unknown number: You left me no choice.

Sands of Time

My heart raced as I read the text again. No choice? What did she mean by that, then it all clicked into place like the fucked-up puzzle it was. Kaitlyn. She was talking about Kaitlyn. I dialed the number; the number I'd swore I'd never call again and waited for her to answer.

"Hello?" her voice sounded like sugar coming through the phone.

"What the fuck did you do?" I hissed as the venom fell from my lips.

"I did what I had to. She needed to know what kinda man she's sleeping with. How many more of us are out there pregnant, Eli? How many of us have you lied to?"

"You are a fucking bitch," I growled before ending the call. "God damn it!" I threw the phone in the passenger seat before punching the dashboard. This was not happening. I was finally where I wanted to be, and it was all falling apart because of something that I wasn't even certain was true.

I threw the car in drive, and sped down the road toward her house. I needed to talk to her, and make her see that this wasn't about her or us, this was about me. I'd finally met the woman that Jackson had been warning me about for months. He told me one of my flings would backfire, and I'd better be careful. I'd waved him off, laughing as I'd led each one of them to my bed, and now I was finally seeing it. I'd made a horrible mistake ever trusting her, and now she was ruining everything.

H. D'Agostino

Chapter 21

Eli

When I reached Kaitlyn's house, I pulled into the driveway and parked. The rain was coming down in buckets, and it was so dark out that it was almost impossible to see. I took a few deep breaths before I flung my door open and made a mad dash to the front porch. There was a small over hang at the door, but other than that no protection from the elements was available. I pounded on the door all the while shouting, "Kait! I know you're in there!" I was met with nothing but silence as I frantically attempted to get her to the door. "Kait!" I slammed harder with my fist, almost bruising my hand.

After a few seconds, I rushed around to the side of the house where I knew her bedroom was. I cupped my hands around my eyes and peered into the window. It was dark, and hard to see, but her bed looked undisturbed. The storm raged as rain soaked my clothes through. My shoes squished like sponges with each step I took, my clothes plastered to me like a second skin. At this point, I gave up running. I was already wet, and as long as I didn't get struck by lightning, I didn't see my night getting worse.

I slopped back to the front of the house, this time stopping at the front window. I wiped the raindrops from where they were dripping off my hair, and cupped my hands again. There she was, lying in a ball on her side on the couch. If it wasn't for the shaking, one would think she was asleep. "Kait!" I pounded on the window, and watched her flinch. "Talk to me, Kait!" I banged again.

Right when I was lifting my hand to hit the glass once more, she slowly started to move. Her feet lowered to the floor as she pushed herself up, and began shuffling toward the door. I rushed back to the small porch, ready to wrap her in my arms and tell her how sorry I was and how much I loved her, but I was met with nothing but the large wooden door.

"Kait," my voice was quieter, but just as desperate. "Please," I begged.

"Go away, Eli," she cried. "I don't want to talk to you."

"Let me explain," I begged. "Just open the door, and we can talk."

"No," her voice was muffled. "Please, just go away."

"I'm not walking away from you, Kait. I love you," I pressed my face to the door hoping that she could feel me. "Please."

"Go home, Eli." I raised my hands to pound on the door once more, but froze. I wasn't getting anywhere. "Please leave."

"I love you, Kait. I always have, and I always will. I'm here when you're ready talk," I kissed my palm, and then pressed it against the door before turning to go back to my car. I'd give her the space she was asking for, but I wasn't giving up, not by a long shot.

oooooooooo

Kaitlyn

I watched his back as he slowly walked back to where he was parked in my driveway. The rain was coming down in sheets. His hair was plastered to his head. He pushed it back, but it was useless. His clothes were dripping he was so wet, and as he shuffled along, his head hung between his shoulders. My chest hurt the farther he walked, and when he got in without even looking back once, my heart cracked again.

I turned, placed my back against the door, and slid to floor much like I'd done in the bakery, only this time I wasn't quiet about it. The tears that had subsided came back full force and as they dripped down my cheeks, I sobbed aloud. The sound was foreign, and I don't remember the last time I hurt this bad. Leaving Henri wasn't as painful as leaving Eli, but I knew that it was over. No matter how much he loved me, he lied to me. He hid this, and the longer I thought about it, the more I wondered what else he was hiding.

oooooooooo

When I awoke this morning, it was quiet in the house. The storm had subsided some time in the early predawn hours of the day. I'd sent a text to Ben late last night letting him know that I wasn't coming in today. After the way I left yesterday, no one was surprised or concerned. I rarely ever took a day off, let alone a sick day. After turning off my phone, I rolled over, pulled the covers over my head. And attempted to go back to sleep. I guess I was fairly successful since I didn't awake until I heard a knock on my door.

At first I thought it might be Eli again, but when I glanced at the clock and saw the time, I knew he had to be at the bar. I wrapped my robe around myself as I shuffled to the door, and peered through the peephole. My heart ached when I saw her. I stepped back and tore the door open only to throw myself into her arms as the tears came back.

"Honey, what's wrong?" she hugged me tight just as she used to when I was a little girl.

"Everything Momma," I sobbed as I clung to her. "It's all falling apart, and I don't know what I should do," I sniffed, rubbed my nose with the back of my hand, and then slowly backed up to allow us into the house.

"What happened? You seemed so happy the other night," she guided me over to the couch, the spot I spent most of yesterday lying in. As I began to tell her all about Tracy and the ambush, she put on me, my mother did what she'd always done when I was little. She marched into my kitchen, and began brewing me a cup of tea. As she carried the steaming mug, and lowered herself onto the couch beside me, she hugged me close and waited. It was just what I needed, someone to talk to that knew all about what I'd been through with Henri. I couldn't go through that again, and certainly not with Eli. Getting over Henri was hard, but getting over Eli would be devastating. My feelings were on a completely different level here.

ooooooooo

Eli

"You look like shit," Jackson sighed as he handed me a beer. "What happened?"

My head swung in his direction as my mouth dropped open, "Tracy happened." We'd come back to my place after work today, and I was currently on a mission to test my liver's limits. Work had sucked, and Kaitlyn still wouldn't talk to me.

"You still didn't tell her, did you?" Jackson rubbed his forehead as he rested his elbows on his knees. "I told you something like this was going to happen."

"Wow!" I jerked my head at his words. "That is really rich coming from you," I threw my head back, letting the alcohol pour down my throat. "I spent years listening to you go on and on about your wife, and how you couldn't tell her the truth because it would ruin everything, and now you're lecturing me?" I jabbed my finger at my chest. "All of this happened before Kaitlyn came back here," I flung my arms out. "How can she be mad at me for something that happened when we weren't together?"

"It's not the same thing," Jackson sighed.

"It is the same thing," I stood and started pacing. "I love her. If I thought telling her about Tracy would help, then I would have. I don't even know if this kid is mine, or if this pregnancy is even real. Why would I put Kaitlyn through all of that if it was nothing?"

"Have you told her that?" he peered up at me from where he was still sitting on the couch.

"How the fuck was I supposed to do that? I stood out in the pouring rain begging her to let me in. She wouldn't even open the door, let alone talk to me," I tipped my head back and polished off the beer all the while turning to stride back to my fridge for another.

"Maybe you didn't try hard enough," Jackson shrugged.

"What else am I supposed to do?" I twisted the top off.

"I don't know, but if you love her as much as you say you do, then you need to try harder. Do more, make a grand gesture of some sort, women love that shit," Jackson waved his hand in the air.

"You're a lot of help," I grumbled, but he was right. If I could just get her to talk to me then maybe she'd see that I was trying to protect her. Tracy can be an evil bitch when she wants to, that's one way that she's nothing like Kaitlyn.

"Think Bro. You grew up with this girl. You know all her little secrets that she keeps buried deep in her heart. You know her schedule, and where all her hideouts are. Use that knowledge to your advantage," he tipped his head to the side in a knowing look.

"Damn straight, I do," I set my half-finished beer on the counter. "She's probably at work now. I need to figure out how to get in her house."

"Now you just sound like a stalker," Jackson chuckled.

"Hey, help me or leave," I pointed to the door.

"Fine. What can I do to help?" he crossed his arms over his chest as he leaned back into the cushions.

"You can find a way I can get into her house," I mumbled as I started making a list.

"That's easy. Use the hide a key from the back patio," he grinned. "Next?"

"How do you know she has a hide a key?" I furrowed my brow as I stopped what I was doing.

"She may have mentioned it to Tessa one time when she was telling her a story about getting locked outside," he chuckled. "I think wine was involved. Don't you think breaking and entering is a bit much?"

"Grand gesture," I rolled my eyes. "I have a plan."

"Care to fill me in?" he patiently waited, but I wasn't giving him details.

"Nope," I kept writing my list. "I may need a few things from the bar, and if it goes well, I won't be in tomorrow night," I folded the paper and stuffed it in my pocket. "Thanks for the beer, but I need you to leave now so I can get started with my planning."

"Good luck," Jackson finished his drink, and then gave a wave before disappearing out the door.

"Thanks," I rubbed my forehead in concentration. "I'm gonna need it."

He laughed as I went to dig through my recipe books. Kaitlyn always complained about being exhausted when she got home each day. I hope a night of pampering relaxes her enough to sit and listen to me. If not, then I'm gonna have a whole lotta Chicken Parm to eat by myself.

Chapter 22

Eli

I got up bright and early this morning with a list of what I want to accomplish before Kaitlyn got home from work for the day. I knew that I needed to do something that would help her out. I remember what it was like when we first opened the bar, and even though she has a staff, she still works herself to the bone. I stopped by the store to grab the groceries I needed, and a few supplies before driving over to her house. I was early, so I parked down the street, and waited for her to leave. I know it sounds bad, but the element of surprise is half my ammo here. There will be a bigger impact, if she doesn't see me until I'm ready, if that makes sense.

I sat there sipping my coffee as I waited, and finally she came outside. She was dressed in a pair of jeans with her coat wrapped tight around her. A fluffy scarf was bundled around her neck, and her Tervis was steaming in her hand. Winter was just around the corner, but she looked as if she was prepared for a blizzard. I glanced down at my own jeans and hoodie and chuckled. She was always snuggling into my side when we were dating, guess that part hasn't changed much either.

After backing out of her driveway, she turned and went in the opposite direction from where I was parked. This was my chance. I cranked the engine, and pulled right in front of the house. This was it. I was almost home free. I climbed out, grabbed the supplies I'd tossed in my trunk, and then set them by the front door. Luckily, Kaitlyn didn't have any nosy neighbors, or I might be explaining myself today.

I crept around to the back gate, and let myself in. There was a rock right beside the red flower pot, just like Jackson mentioned. When I lifted it, there was the little silver key and my way in. I grinned as I wrapped my fingers around it and went back toward the front door. It slid right into the lock, and I heard the click when I turned the knob. I gave myself a little fist pump before grabbing the bags I'd set on the porch.

After carrying everything inside, I went out the back door and replaced the key. I didn't want to forget and have Kaitlyn need it one day. I set my bags on the counter, and went work. I started in the master bathroom. I scrubbed, sprayed, and mopped every surface with cleaner leaving the room smelling like Lysol. When I finished, I went into her bedroom. The covers were in giant pile in the middle of the bed. I began straightening them before grabbing the loose clothes and tossing them in the hamper. I thought about doing the laundry, but I know that most women have all kinds of rules on what goes where. "Don't put this in the dryer. Make sure you separate this. This is dry clean only. This had a stain." I've heard Tessa yell a few of those at Jackson, and I don't want to give Kaitlyn anymore reasons to be mad at me.

When I'm finished making the bed, I go in search of the vacuum cleaner. After opening a few closets, I find it. I started at the back of the house, and made my way to the front. The living room was probably the messiest. There were magazines piled haphazardly on the coffee table, and throw pillows and a blanket laying on the couch. An empty wine glass was sitting by a laptop on an ottoman, and don't get me started on the number tissues I found. I remembered seeing them the other night when I came by, so I just quickly picked them up. I'm sure I deserve the skeeved out feeling that it gave me. I'm a bit of a neat freak, so cleaning this place up actually made me feel better. When I finished, I took out the trash, and then proceeded to plan out dinner.

I wasn't sure what Kaitlyn would have as far as utensils, but I brought my own knives. If you have ever met a chef, then you know that their knives are scared. You don't touch another chef's knife and you sure as shit don't ask to borrow it. I brought three of my own, and as I placed my supplies on the counter, I began heating a pot on the stove. I make my marinara sauce from scratch, and it takes a while. I like to let it simmer for a few hours so that all the flavors can mix together.

Once I got that taken care of, I put the wine in the fridge, and began slicing up my chicken. I had the pasta all ready to boil, and was pretty much set. After surveying my surroundings, I decided to watch a bit of tv while I waited. I had about an hour to burn before I needed to get ready for Kait, and I was exhausted.

ooooooooo

Kaitlyn

Today has been a long day. It hasn't been bad, just long and I've been putting off talking to Eli. I know I have to, but I don't want to. I spent most of the afternoon convincing myself that I had to go by the bar tonight and hear his side of this, but I just didn't want to. I've been with someone that's not honest, and I really don't want to go down that path again. I don't even want to entertain the idea. I've been sitting here in the parking lot of Anchor Bay for the last ten minutes trying to force myself to go inside.

Just as I was starting to open my door, Jackson comes out. I froze, hoping he didn't see me, but I was too late. He was heading right for my car. He stopped beside it, and knocked on the window. I sighed as I lowered it. "He's not here if you're wondering," he placed his arm on the top of the car and leaned down. "Took the day off."

"Oh," I pressed my lips together. I don't know if that feeling in my chest was relief or hurt. Everything hurt now, and as much anger as I had toward him, the hurt was worse. "Thanks," I glanced up at him and he nodded. He didn't say anything after that, just turned and went back inside. I rolled my window back up, and sat there for a few more minutes before backing up and heading home.

oooooooo

When I pulled into my driveway, I sat there for a few minutes just listening to the radio. The song playing seemed fitting, and I couldn't bring myself to turn it off and get out. The guy was singing to his lover about forgiveness. He was begging her to forgive him, almost pleading with her. He tells her that he doesn't know what he's doing, and he loves her so much that he just can't walk away. He can't give up, but he's confused and lost and needs her help. Tears spring to my eyes because it sounds just like Eli. He's been begging me to talk to him, to forgive him, but I don't know if I can.

The song ends, and I slowly climb out of my car. As I'm walking to the door, I get this weird feeling that washes over me. It's like when you're out and you know someone's watching you, but you don't want to turn around and bust them. I feel it now, but no one's around. As I push the door open, I can smell something coming from inside, and then I see a shadow.

"Don't freak out," his voice warns as he appears in the doorway. Eli is standing there in a gray sweater and jeans. He's got an apron tied around his waist, and he's barefoot. My eyes scan him from top to bottom as my mouth opens and closes as few times.

"What? How?" I motion to the house as I attempt to grab my purse before it falls the rest of the way from my arm. I shake my head to clear it, but it doesn't help.

"I made dinner. I thought we could talk," he cringes like he's guilty before stepping to the side, and letting me in. "Would you like a glass of wine?"

"Sure," I nibble my lip as I toss my purse on the couch. It takes me a minute to notice, but the room is straightened up.

"Here," he comes back with a glass of red and motions down the hall. "Go get comfortable."

I close my eyes and take a few deep breaths, willing the tears to stay away. When I opened them, he was just standing there, smiling at me. I sighed before heading toward my bedroom.

When I pushed open the door, I almost dropped my wine. My bed was made, the floor picked up, one of my scented candles was lit on my dresser. I closed the door, and then sat on the bed. He did this, but why? I quickly stripped out of my bakery clothes, and tossed them in the hamper. Any other day, and I probably would have thrown them on the floor, but after all the work he did I just couldn't. I grabbed a pair of leggings and a sweatshirt, and then quickly rushed into the bathroom. I wanted to freshen up, but I skidded to a stop when I smelled the cleaner. He'd been in here too. My heart melted a little at the thought of Eli on his hands and knees scrubbing my bathroom.

By the time I got back out to the living room, Eli was plating whatever he'd cooked. It smelled delicious, and my stomach growled in agreement. "I hope you're hungry," he smiled as he placed the plates on the table.

"I'm starving," I sighed as I approached the table. I stopped in my tracks when I saw what he'd fix. "I can't believe you remember," my voice trembled. It was too much, but perfect all at the same time. Chicken Parmigiana was the meal we had on our first date when we were kids. Every time we celebrated anything significant, that was what we ate. We had sparkling juice the first time, but now were able to have the real thing.

"I remember everything, Kait. I remember the red dress you wore, and how it matched the table cloth. I remember the way you fixed your hair. I remember that despite being full, you still shared a piece of cheesecake with me. I remember dancing on the beach to my ipod. I remember how your dad flashed the porch lights at us when we took too long to say goodnight, and" he came around to where I was standing and reached for my hand, entwining our fingers, "I remember what it felt like to kiss you the first time." He leaned forward and pressed a light kiss to my cheek before releasing me to pull out my chair. "Have a seat," he motioned before moving to sit across from me.

"I know you think that I'm not taking us seriously, but I am," he shook his napkin out and placed it in his lap. "I'm hopelessly in love with you, Kait. I know that I have a lot of explaining to do, but you have to know that I love you."

I nodded as I pushed my fork around on my plate. "I know you do, but is it enough?" He started to talk, but I held my hand up stopping him, "I've been married to someone who wasn't honest. I can't do that again Eli, I won't." My eyes started to tear up, but I pushed them back. "I love you too. I think I always have, but I need you to talk to me, no matter what. I can't have you hiding things that you think will upset me. If you do, then I can't do this." I stared at the pasta on my plate.

I heard his chair scrape, and before I knew it, he was beside me. "I'll tell you whatever you wanna know. Ask me," he grabbed my hand.

"Did you sleep with that woman?" I swallowed and waited.

"Yes."

"Did you like it?" I pressed my lips together to keep from crying.

"It was sex, Kait." He sighed.

"That's not what I asked," I turned to look at him. "Did you like it?"

"Did I get what I needed from her, yes." He stared at me, waiting.

"Is the baby yours?" I felt a single tear roll down my cheek.

"No. Maybe. Fuck, I don't know. We used condoms, Kait. I mean nothing's a hundred percent, but I really don't think it's mine," he tugged on my arm as I started to pull away.

"Are there more?" I felt my voice crack.

"More what? Women?" He stood, and took a step back. "Let me ask you this. Did you date while you were in Paris? Did you sleep with other men? After Henri, did you?"

"Why does that matter?" I cried. I was trying so hard to stay calm, but the longer I sat here talking to him the more I saw her under him. Her touching him. Her kissing him. I had no rights to him when they were together, but jealousy was an evil bitch and she didn't care.

"Exactly!" he flung his arms out to the side. "Does it bother me? Fuck yes it does. I don't want to think about you with anyone else, but I know there have been others. We haven't been together in ten years. I can't expect you to revirginize yourself. I would like to think that we've grown up, and can think about this as adults." He ran his hands through his hair, and tugged at the ends. "I love you, Kait. I want this to work, but it won't if you hold things, I did in the past against me. You weren't here when Tracy and I were together."

"I just...ugh!" I slammed my fist against the table causing the dishes to rattle. "I hate her so much."

"Believe me, I do too," he groaned as he paced back over to his chair. "I wish none of this was happening, but it is, and there's nothing I can do about it right now. The baby's due in four months. I'm going to ask for a paternity test as soon as it arrives. All we can do is wait until then."

"Then what?" I sat back in my chair and watched him. I wanted him to be honest. I wanted to know that letting him back in wasn't going to completely shatter me.

"If it's mine, I'll help. If it's not, then she's got a lot of explaining to do. I don't love her. I don't want her. I'm with you, that is if you'll have me," he folded his hands on the table and stared intently at me.

"I'm just scared, Eli," I murmured.

"I know you are, but aren't we worth the risk? Aren't we something you'd like to take that leap on?" he reached across the table and squeezed my hand. "Don't you want to see what we can be like without all the secrets?" He smiled and licked his lips. "I think our hourglass has only begun to drain. We still have plenty of time left."

Chapter 23

Kaitlyn

Tonight, had been a bit overwhelming to say the least. After we finished eating, Eli drew me a bath, and then proceeded to clean the kitchen and do the dishes. I've been sitting here in the tub for the last half hour just listening to him bustle around my house. The hot water feels good on my tired muscles, and knowing that I don't have any cleaning to do is helping me relax. I don't remember the last time I had a bath. Most night, I toss my clothes on the floor, jump in the shower for a quick 'rinse and run', and then crash into bed. The nights that I have time to do other things on are usually spent at Eli's. I slide lower into the hot water as I hear a knock at the door.

"How's it going in here?" Eli's head peers around the corner, and he looks like a little kid asking permission to come in.

"It's great," I sigh as I dribble bubbles over my chest. Eli's eyes dilate slightly and his Adam's apple bob. "Something wrong?"

"No. Not at all. I'm glad you're comfortable," he smiled. His voice sounded strained, and he started to back up and leave me.

"You can come in, if you like," I shifted to sit up slightly, and my breasts almost came out of the water. He hissed, and the grip he had on the door jamb made his knuckles white.

"I'm trying to be good here, Kait. If I come closer, I don't think I can." He sighed as he gripped the back of his neck.

"I thought that this is what you wanted," I bent my knee so it came out the water and bubbles sloshed over the edge of the tub.

"Tonight, was about you, not this," he groaned, his restraint failing, but I couldn't help it. I needed to push him. I needed to know that what he'd said during dinner was the truth. My brain knew she didn't matter, but my heart was having a hard accepting it.

"I don't want you to be good," I murmured. "I want you to show me how you feel. You've told me, now show me." I lifted my scrubby, and ran the soap across my chest. As I let it trail down between my breast and below the water, I sighed. "I really need you to show me."

"Fuck it!" he growled as he ripped his sweater over his head and tossed it to the floor. As he rushed into the bathroom, he stepped out of his shoes and released his belt. The jingling of the buckle caused me to look up just in time to see him free himself. "Stand up," he commanded, and my nipples puckered with anticipation. As I stood, he shoved his jean over his hips, and lifted me into his arms. My legs wrapped around his waist at the same time his mouth crashed into mine.

"I love you so much, Kait. There aren't even words to describe how much I need you," he turned us, and sat me on the edge of the vanity. "You're a little slippery and wet," he murmured as he stepped between my legs. "I don't want to drop you," he pumped himself a few times before guiding his cock between my thighs. My head fell back as my eyes rolled closed, and Eli went to work showing me just how much he needed me.

ooooooooo

"How did you get in here?" We were currently curled up in my bed. Our legs tangled together, my head resting on his shoulder as I drew lazy circles with my index finger in the smattering of chest hair, I'd become fond of.

"I used a key," he chuckled. When he didn't elaborate, I gently kicked him. "Ouch," he pulled his foot back. "Jackson told me where you hide your key. I used it," he shrugged causing my head to bob.

"Where did you park? I mean, I should have seen your car. Wait! Did you walk all this way?" I lifted my head to stare at him.

"Yeah Kait. I walked four miles with three bags of groceries, and all my cooking supplies." He rolled his eyes and I smacked his chest. "I'm parked down the street," he laughed. "I was afraid you wouldn't come inside if you knew I was here. Jackson told me to do something grand, something that you'd like. How'd I do?" he grinned.

"You got laid, didn't you?" I tipped my head to the side as I pressed my lips together.

"Oh yeah," one hand pulled me closer causing me to almost lie on top of him as the other squeezed my ass cheek. "But seriously Kait, I meant what I said. All of it. I love you. I want you. I'll take responsibility. I'll be a good dad if that's what all this means, but I will not be with her. I hope you understand," he pulled me in for a slow soft kiss.

"I do now, but you can explain it more if you like," I teased before burying my face in the crook of his neck.

This was us. This is where we should have been all those years ago. I don't know why the universe chose to separate us when it did, but everything happens for a reason right? If being apart for ten years meant coming back to a lifetime of happiness, then I guess it was worth

Sands of Time

it. Eli was right. Our hourglass still had plenty of sand left in it. Our love would withstand the sands of time.

Epilogue

4 years later

Eli

They say the older you get; the faster time seems to go. I'd like to say they're wrong, but I'd be lying. The time between Kaitlyn moving back and the day we said 'I do' seemed like a blur. One moment we were trying to get our footing, and the next... we were moving in together. I knew when I saw her on the sidewalk all those years ago that we would end up here, I just didn't know all the obstacles we'd have to dodge to get here.

It turns out that fatherhood isn't as bad as I once thought it would be. Having a son has been the best thing in my life besides marrying my soulmate, that is. It's even better when you plan it. Tracy is not my son's mother, in case you were wondering. Right after she had her baby, I requested a paternity test, and wouldn't you know? It wasn't mine. When the paperwork came in the mail with the big black letters across it stating "You are not the father", I celebrated by asking Kait to marry me.

Another fun fact: Turns out I'm pretty good at making babies. Kaitlyn went off her birth control that night, and six weeks later the stick turned pink. I thought I'd be scared, but I was happy, ecstatic even. I knew we'd make great parents, and it gave me an even better reason to rush the wedding. By rush, I mean we got married right here on the beach just four months later. Kaitlyn didn't want to look pregnant on our wedding day, and I wasn't about to wait until after the baby came.

The morning that Xavier Eric Baker came into the world was both the happiest and scariest day of my life. The minutes seems to slow to almost a snail's pace as I wore a track in the hospital room floor. My beautiful wife called me every ugly name known to man as she pushed our son from her body. I watched in fascination as the nurses cleaned him up, and finally handed him over to me. "Here ya go Dad," was terrifying to hear at the moment, but now when my little guys yells, "Dad!" I feel nothing but pride, most of time. I'm sure as the years go by there will be days that I want to scream at him, moments that he makes me so mad I nearly lose my shit, and days were I fear the world will eat him alive, but right now we're enjoying our afternoon on the beach.

ooooooooo

"Do again, Daddy?" Xav tugged on my hand to get my attention. We're standing in the shallow water on the beach, and every time a wave comes, Xav leaps over it, with my help of course.

"Ok. Ready?" I stand behind him holding him by both hands. As the wave rolls in, I lift him in the air. He kicks his little feet as the water splashes around my calves spraying us both.

"Again?" he squeals as he tugs at my grip.

"We've been at this for a while, Buddy. Let's go eat some lunch first. Mommy's hungry, and she probably misses us," I start to pull him toward Kaitlyn. It took a minute to convince that he was hungry, but he soon gave in.

"What's for lunch?" I smiled down at where she was sitting on a blanket under a beach umbrella.

"Ham sandwich for you, and PB&J for Xan the Man," she handed me two sandwiches wrapped in cling wrap.

"Yum," I sighed as I opened mine. "All this sun and water is making me hungry. Wish I could say the same for him," I nodded my head to where Xavier was currently filling a bucket with sand. The kid never stopped unless his was sleeping.

"He won't starve himself," Kaitlyn shrugged as she took a bite of her own sandwich.

"How do you know that?" I furrowed my brow.

"He's a kid. When he gets hungry enough, he'll eat," she rolled her eyes.

Sands of Time

"You're so good at all this mom stuff," I mumbled around a bite of sandwich.

"Mom stuff?" she wrinkled her nose.

"Yeah. The eating and napping, and all that," I finished my sandwich and balled up the cling wrap.

"You're pretty good too," she smiled. "I know you doubt yourself sometimes, Eli, but you really are a good dad. He's proof," she nodded her head at Xav.

"Sometimes I wonder," I sighed. "I mean," I grinned at her "I knew what I was doing when we made him, but now sometimes I feel a little lost."

"We all do," she smiled me. "You are right though," she turned and began rummaging through the picnic basket, "you do know what you're doing." As I stared at her in confusion, she grabbed my hand and placed a small box in it. "Open it," she smiled.

It was then that time seemed to stop. Cradled in some tissue paper was a small white stick with two pink lines. "Is this what I think it is?" I blinked a few times as my eyes danced between her and box.

"Are you ok with that?" she nibbled her lip. "I mean Xav's only two."

"I'm great with that," I pulled her in for a hug and murmured in her ear "I love you."

"I love you too," she kissed me lightly before pulling back and looking over at Xav. "You think he's handful, what if this one's a girl," both our eyes dropped her stomach.

"Nope, not even gonna think about it," I shook my head as I leaned back on my elbows on the sand.

It was in that moment that the sands of time sped up once again. The grains of sand would soon run faster through our hourglass, and I would spend every minute of it trying to make time stand still. For every moment is precious, and something you can never get back.

The End

Sands of Time Playlist

Never Be the Same- Camila Cabello

I Was Jack- Jake Owen

Comeback- Kane Brown

Hello Summer- Danielle Bradbury

Something Tonight- Taylor Acorn

Dammit- Jana Kramer

Speechless- Dan + Shay

Here Tonight- Brett Young

What Do I Do- Taylor Acorn

Think & Drive- Seth Ennis

Best Shot- Jimmie Allen

Put It In A Song- Taylor Acorn

This Is It- Scotty McCreery

Bring It On Over- Billy Currington

Let You Love Me- Rita Ora

Happier- Marshmello

Other Works by H. D'Agostino

The Witness Series

Being Nobody

Becoming Somebody

Promise Me Tomorrow

Say You Remember

Below the Surface

Crash and Burn

The Broken Series

Irreparably Broken

Saving Us

My Broken Angel

Broken Pieces

The Shattered Series

Destined

Shattered

Sands of Time
Restored

Renewed

Fated

The Sutter Family Series

Catching Raindrops

Trusting You

Finding the Green Room

Teaching Cayden

The Cook Brothers Series

Walking Among the Cherry Trees

Beyond the Cherry Trees

Before the Cherry Trees

The Second Chances Series

Unbreak Me

The Boy Next Door

The One That Got Away

H. D'Agostino

Inside Out

Fallen From Grace

The Family Next Door

Standalones

Privileged

Beautiful Goodbye

Home for the Holidays

Pieces of Forever

Acknowledgements

I never know what to say for these. There are so many people that help me along the way to make my stories the best they can be. I have a great team.

Thank you, Angie, for always being honest with me about my characters. I never have to worry about releasing a bad story. You tell it like it is, whether it's to tell me it sucks, or that its awesome. I know my heroes sometimes push your buttons, but you know you love it. Why else would you keep coming back for more?

Tabitha... where do I start? The endless torture? Sending you half a book? Teasing you relentlessly? It's all part of being inducted into the cool kid's club. Thank you for your endless support, and not showing up at my door step to kill me when I push you to you limits.

Melinda... thank you for putting up with all the shenanigans that Angie and I put you through. You're the voice of reason when we plot our activities. You balance out the crazy.

Kellie... my most awesome editor. Thank you for continuing to work with me, and fast at that. I always know that I'll get a quality product back.

Cassy... thank you for another beautiful cover, and formatting job.

Thank you to everyone who has shared, tweeted, and posted about Eli and Kate. I appreciated your help and love the fact that you love my books.

About the Author

Heather D'Agostino is an avid reader turned Bestselling Author of the Contemporary Romance Series The Broken Series, The Shattered Series, The Second Chances Series, The Cook Brothers Series, and Romantic Suspense series The Witness Series.

She attended the University of North Carolina at Charlotte where she received a Bachelor's of Arts in Elementary Education with a minor in Mathematics.

She currently lives in Central New York with her husband, two children, two dogs, and three cats. When she's not writing she can usually be found at the dance studio, soccer field, or one of the many other places that she plays 'Supermom'.

You can follow her here:

Facebook: www.facebook.com/H.DAgostino.Author

Twitter: @hdagostino001

Instagram: @hdagostino001

Website: http://hdagostinobooks.weebly.com

Reader Group/ Street Team on Facebook:

Heather's Hotties:

https://www.facebook.com/groups/877863252256341/

Goodreads: https://www.goodreads.com/author/show/7034328.Heather_D_Agostino

I love hearing from my readers, so please feel free to reach out.

Sands of Time

Made in the USA
Middletown, DE
18 July 2019